Secrets from Myself

DCB

**Canada Council
for the Arts** **Conseil des Arts
du Canada** 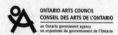 ONTARIO ARTS COUNCIL
CONSEIL DES ARTS DE L'ONTARIO
an Ontario government agency
un organisme du gouvernement de l'Ontario

🍁 Canadian   Patrimoine
Heritage   canadien   **Canadä**

The publisher gratefully acknowledges the support of the Canada Council for the
Arts and the Ontario Arts Council for its publishing program. We acknowledge the
financial support of the Government of Canada through the Canada Book Fund
(CBF) for our publishing activities, and the Government of Ontario through the
Ontario Media Development Corporation, an agency of the Ontario Ministry of
Culture, and the Ontario Book Publishing Tax Credit Program.

LIBRARY AND ARCHIVES CANADA CATALOGUING IN PUBLICATION

Hart, Christine, 1978–, author
Secrets from myself / Christine Hart.

Issued in print and electronic formats.
ISBN 978-1-77086-490-0 (softcover). — ISBN 978-1-77086-491-7 (html)

I. Title.

PS8615.A773668S43 2017   jC813'.6   C2016-907296-7
C2016-907297-5

United States Library of Congress Control Number: 2016945337

Cover design: angeljohnguerra.com
Interior text design: Tannice Goddard, bookstopress.com

Printed and bound in Canada.
Manufactured by Friesens in Altona, Manitoba, Canada in June, 2017.

DANCING CAT BOOKS
An imprint of Cormorant Books Inc.
10 ST. MARY STREET, SUITE 615, TORONTO, ONTARIO, M4Y 1P9
www.dancingcatbooks.com
www.cormorantbooks.com

In Memory of Harvinder Kaur Gakhal
May 16, 1978 – April 5, 1996

Prologue

I can barely see into the dimly lit room ahead through the small holes in the wall of Sanjay's trunk. The clunk-thud of metal on metal signifies that I am locked in by a thick padlock. I am cramped and the fabric lining on the pine panels adds no comfort. This is okay, though. We are almost there and my confinement is part of our plan.

I have been living behind a fake wall in Sanjay and his father's cabin for almost two months. Now I welcome these brief hours of more intense imprisonment. This box is how I got on board and it is how I will get into Canada. Once this part is done, and Sanjay is safely into Vancouver, we will run from his father and start our lives.

"Akasha?" Sanjay whispers, his lips brushing against the holes in the trunk. "Can you breathe? Will you be all right?"

"Yes," I whisper back. "Do not worry. And do not talk. We cannot risk it."

A knock on the door draws Sanjay's attention. I hear two men bark something in Japanese. Sanjay has learned some of their language, but there has been no chance for me.

Sanjay answers in halting, awkward Japanese words. I hope everything is all right. I have to believe everything is fine. Sanjay leaves to follow them and his cabin door slams shut.

It seems like hours, but Sanjay finally returns, this time with his father. My presence is a secret from Mr. Hasan most of all. To the crew of this ship, I would be a mere stowaway. To Sanjay's father, my discovery would represent his son's ultimate disobedience. Mr. Hasan has already declined permission for Sanjay to choose his own bride in a love match. They have come to Canada for the marriage Mr. Hasan arranged for his son when Sanjay was a boy. But we have other plans.

"Why do they not allow us to dock, father?" asks Sanjay.

"This is exactly what I feared, but we will put up a fight," says Mr. Hasan. "You are ready to go at a moment's notice?"

"Yes sir. I am ready, just as you instructed," says Sanjay. The fear in his voice is unmistakable. A problem with port authorities is good, though, as it will provide an easy explanation for any anxiety Sanjay cannot conceal.

"Come," says Mr. Hasan briskly. "We need to find your uncle as well."

They leave the room. A few moments later, the door opens again. I strain to see the figures through my air holes. Two men speaking in hushed Japanese are looking around the room. They seem to be looking for something specific.

The gaze of one man comes to rest on me — that is, on Sanjay's trunk. The other man looks over and they both walk towards the trunk. They share a laugh and I can feel myself being lifted. One man mutters something I think might be a string of curse words, based on his tone.

As they carry me out the door and up a stairwell, my excitement grows. The problem with the Canadian port must have been resolved. In hours — maybe even minutes — I will be reunited with Sanjay and we will run away together. We've planned for so long and the moment is finally here.

Sounds coming from the deck do not support my interpretation. Men are arguing. Hindi, Punjabi, Japanese, English; I can hear a crowd of voices in several languages and all of them are angry.

"There is no excuse! We are here legally," shouts a man in Hindi.

"— won't stand for this!" yells another.

"We are British citizens! You can't do this!" calls out another man in English.

"This is what we think of your regulations," says another protestor in English with a very thick accent.

I am straining to make out other statements, but a sudden lurch catches my breath. The trunk is being swung back and forth. The men carrying me are getting ready to throw it. Something is wrong.

The trunk is suddenly free, sailing through the air. Yells and cheers fade as I feel the arc of my descent. I look out through my air holes straining to see a cart or straw or some possible soft landing.

Oh god, we are still at SEA! The trunk hits the ocean with a CRACK-SLAP. Water starts to leak in through the seams at the corners. I can feel the icy wet seeping into my backside and onto my feet. The air holes spray water in my face.

I have once chance; I *must* burst the trunk! I press my back against the short wall behind me and push with my feet against the opposite end of the box. Ice water starts to rush in. I push harder and harder still.

Muffled snaps go off around me and the top of the trunk caves in. The water, the fabric, and the wood are all suffocating me! I kick and flail despite the body-shocking cold.

A salty taste fills my mouth, but I am free of the debris, weighed down now only by my wet clothes. I open my eyes to see murky brown that stings instantly.

Eyes shut, I kick up and up until I emerge on the surface. I am alive! The ship is many yards away. I look back and forth between the ship and the slimy posts of the dock nearby. The decision has to be made now.

I start towards the shore, looking up to see if anyone on the ship or the dock has noticed me. No faces meet my gaze. Angry men shout at each other. They throw bricks, coal, and whatever else they can find with enough weight to project at their enemies.

I reach the dock, find a ladder, and hang on, hidden from view. Before I climb, I need to think. I have to get out of these cold, wet clothes. I have nothing, nobody, and nowhere to go.

The late spring weather of May in Canada is still cold, it seems — in the ocean at least. I can stand a few more minutes. What is my plan? There is nothing for it. I must climb up and try to hide while I dry.

I climb onto a dock surrounded by net-covered crates. This is not a point of entry for passengers and there are very few people around. I curl up into a space between the crates which conceals me from the shore. My brown sari, which I have been wearing to hide with ease on ship, is still working to camouflage me. I may blend in long enough to dry off.

All the shouting has stopped. The sun is setting, painting the sky a beautiful hot orange fringed with pink and purple clouds. The cold is not so bad now, or I am numb. I can make it until morning. I rest against the side of a crate, nestling my head into a gap in the netting.

I watch the sky drain of its warm color. Stars pop out on a wall of navy blue and I can see lights across the water in the distance. The murmur of regular port noise dies down and all I can hear is the ocean lapping against the pillars below as sleep takes me.

Chapter 1

My hospital room is too bright. I look over at the mirror on the wall beside me. I note a twinge of cool green in my messy sandy hair. Combined with my light blue eyes, I look gaunt in the unnatural fluorescence. Only my long eyelashes and button nose rescue me from looking undead. I turned the cursed lights off a few hours ago and a nurse came in minutes afterwards grumbling about security and turned them back on. I'm waiting for her shift to end so I can turn them back off. The window at the far end of the room lets in enough light for me to read and that's all I need. My diary is my lifeline now that I'm stuck in the Adolescent Psychiatric Inpatient Unit at BC Children's Hospital.

माँ, मुझे आपकी बहुत याद आती है। क्या आपको मेरे विचार और प्राथना सुनाई देते है? आपके बिना, संजय ही मेरा सबकुछ था। मै उसे भी खो नही सकती थी। मुझे कोशिशि तो करनी थी। और अब गड़बड़ हो गयी है।

Mother, I miss you so much. Can you hear my thoughts and prayers? Without you, Sanjay was all I had. I couldn't lose him too. I had to try. And now it's such a mess.

Sanjay, where are you? Why have you not come for me?
You could jump overboard in the dead of night and swim
to shore like I did. Have you changed your mind? I am so
lost in this city. I have lost count of the days. The nights
are long and dark. But I wait for you. Still waiting.
I think I will be waiting forever.

I spend several minutes thinking about this passage — again. I've read it dozens of times. The first time I discovered this entry, I thought someone had played a trick on me. Not just because I found another language — which I later learned was Hindi — but because I had no memory of writing it. I showed it to Mom and she thought I was playing a trick on her. I searched online until I found a description that fit: automatic writing.

The short paragraphs made no sense, even the second one I could read. I had no idea who Sanjay was. Shortly after first reading it, I had a dream about being thrown off a boat in an antique steamer trunk. A boy had called me Akasha. I told Mom about the dream and she dismissed me again.

It wasn't the first time I'd been someone else in a dream. But everyone has dreams where they're someone else. I wouldn't have ditched my mom at a Surrey gas station and hopped a city bus over nothing more than a strange dream and a single cryptic diary passage. There have been other dreams in which I'm Akasha and there have been other diary entries in her writing. This morning, however, I'll write more of my own story.

July 3

I'm trying not to be angry that I'm in a hospital bed. I'm not sick — in any conceivable way. I'm trying not to be angry at Mom for thinking I'm crazy, or at Bryce's parents for calling the police when they found me. I wasn't going to try living in their basement. I just needed a place to stop and regroup before going downtown. I should have gone straight downtown to find the Port of Vancouver. But I was too scared to go alone. I thought Bryce would come with me. He's the only person other than Mom who knows about my dreams and my diary. He doesn't think I'm nuts. Of course, I still haven't told Bryce he looks an awful lot like the boy on the steamship from my dreams. I don't trust it myself. I've had a crush on Bryce for years. Why my brain inserted him into one of my visions is beyond my understanding.

I close my diary for a moment to think. I pull my thick tousled hair back and give it a single twist to keep it all behind me. It has been almost a month since Dr. MacDonald scheduled my visit to the Child & Youth Mental Health Offices. In our first visit, he told me unconsciously copying someone else's writing is called cryptomnesia. I told him that wasn't what happened to me and he eyed me carefully. During our third visit he asked if I knew why my mother thought I was mentally ill. She had told him her big secret about my "weird speech" and my "funny moments," which she originally took for epilepsy, until several rounds of testing ruled that out. As a single mother, my mom paid a lot of attention to my physical, and more importantly to her, psychological, well-being. So when I told her I believed I had been a stowaway on a ship from India in a past life, the first thing she did was make an appointment with the next available child psychologist. Where we live in Nelson—well, the Kootenays in general—child psychologists are a bit hard to find.

I don't know if I should regret confiding in my mother about Akasha. She had already seen me "tune out" and talk about times and places I couldn't possibly remember. It started when I was around six years old, before I had the sense to keep my weirdness to myself. Mom even took the precaution of transferring me from one elementary school to another, which is a big deal when you live in a tiny mountain town. She waited until I was old enough for a fresh start to be useful. I have to give her credit for that at least. I learned to keep my mouth shut and be as boring as plain oatmeal.

Then again, if I hadn't said anything to Mom about Akasha, she never would have taken me to see Dr. MacDonald. I wouldn't have heard phrases like Dissociative Identity Disorder and Borderline Personality Disorder. I would never have managed a trip to

Vancouver on my own, which was actually my chance
to see my best friend Bryce again and find out about
Akasha for myself.

Bryce moved to Vancouver when his father, Professor
Mann, got a job offer with the BC Institute of Tech-
nology. He was my friend when we were little because
he lived two doors down from me. He stayed friends
with me after I switched schools, knowing I was a "weird"
kid. When I woke up one morning and realized I had
a crush on him, there was no way I was going to tell
him. He was one of the cute boys. Still is. He has dark
hair, light brown eyes, and warm brown skin. He's even
starting to grow tall.

When Bryce told me he was leaving town, it was like a
punch in the gut. Then my dreams kicked into overdrive
and I found Hindi in my diary, along with a passage I
never wrote. I felt like my life had been turned upside
down, shaken, and then tilted on its side.

By the time Mom was driving into the Lower Mainland, I hoped with every fiber of my being that I'd get
a chance to bolt, and that I'd be able to find Bryce. He
came from an Indian family that had immigrated and
I thought he might be interested in hearing about my
dreams of the steamship. Once I was on that bus in Surrey,
I texted him for directions. I told him it was top secret.

As my escape from Mom and refuge at Bryce's house
replays in my mind, my phone buzzes on the bedside
table. It's Bryce. I swipe the glass to read.

I'm sorry. You would have been caught with or without me. And my parents would have killed me. Twice. Don't hate me.

What? It was Bryce? Traitor!

Chapter 2

I pick my phone out of the lined plastic waste bin I threw it into. I wipe the glass, checking for chips and cracks with a flush of embarrassment that rises up from my gut to my cheeks. I'm always quick to anger — and equally quick to feel remorse.

I hadn't expected Bryce to cover for me. Not for long, anyway. I know I put him in a ridiculous position, showing up after I'd run away from my mom.

I know you had no choice. I'm not mad. It was a stupid thing to do anyway, I tap intently, hit Send, and start tapping again. *Trapped in hospital. Could use a visitor.*

A few minutes pass while I scroll through Tumblr photos, waiting, hoping to smooth things over.

What room are you in?

I send Bryce directions to BC Children's Hospital and to my room specifically. The facility may be one of a kind, but I'm betting my friend hasn't had to trek out to this part of Vancouver in the four months he's been here.

Bryce won't be visiting until after dinner. Mom won't be back for hours either. I know wandering the halls will get me in trouble with that uptight nurse. I need something to occupy my mind. My diary waits for me to rescue it from the hospital nightstand drawer next to my bed, along with a mercifully fresh pen. My precious book is trapped in a weird room too. Writing will make me feel better, but if it doesn't I'll still feel that sense of relief I can get no other way.

I flip to a fresh page. The soft blue lines on crisp white paper look so inviting and … I draw a blank. Writer's block? This hardly ever happens to me. Although, most of the time I pick up my diary because an idea grabs me, not because I'm imprisoned somewhere and bored out of my skull. I close my eyes to think. Nothing comes. But the relief from the fluorescent light is sweet. I let my tired lids stay closed a moment longer. It's not even lunch time and I feel as though I could drift off to sleep.

The sound of pen scratching on paper catches my attention and I open my eyes. Where did THIS come from? The two empty pages I closed my eyes on are now full!

We have finally left Punjab behind and the voyage has begun. I will never see India again. The first part was easy. I used what little money I had to buy a ticket on Sanjay's train and hide well away from him and his father. But it was a near thing, my sneaking aboard Sanjay's ship in Calcutta. I was terrified, but ready. I hid in the back corner of the boiler room as planned. And waited. And waited.

When I heard a voice whisper, "Akasha? Are you here?" it was a thrilling moment. I felt all had been achieved. Sanjay had waited for his father to fall asleep and carried the contents of his largest trunk down here, to exchange for me.

We risked a moment's embrace before we stole back to his cabin. Relieved to find Mr. Hasan still asleep, Sanjay showed me the dressing screen at the back of the cabin. This is where I would be released to spend my nights. Days would have to be spent shut in the trunk, or otherwise hidden on the ship. Sanjay vowed with all his worth to find me reliable hiding places so I would not have to spend endless hours in the trunk. We will be changing ships in a matter of days and I will be confined again until Sanjay can assess our surroundings once more. I pray Sanjay can carry the trunk alone or that no one finds it too heavy.

Being confined in this wood and cloth cage is the most secure and suffocating feeling I have ever known. Until we arrive in Vancouver, this trunk is the safest place for me. I will tolerate it as much as possible. If it were anyone other than Sanjay outside this cage, I would scream. For him, I keep silent. And I know that Mr. Hasan will have me thrown overboard if he doesn't toss me out to sea with his own hands.

I must force myself to stop thinking of the passage of time while I am confined. I am hopeful that Mr. Hasan will give Sanjay more space, now that he believes his son's fate is sealed. It is a silly thing to think of, having *space on a crowded steamship. I am better served by hoping Sanjay can locate safe hiding spots. Perhaps an accomplice — or two — who may be trusted. I can only leave those details in Sanjay's capable hands.*

Is this for REAL? Did I just write this? HOW? I look down at the blue ballpoint pen in my hand. I look back to the freshly written text in front of me. It's not possible.

Re-reading the story sends my heart racing and my brain spinning. What is this nonsense? I need a clue, a real live lead, not more about being locked in a trunk! What's the name of the ship?

No, wait, there is a lead here. The ship left a place called Calcutta. But I still need more. The images from my dreams are still fresh in my mind. Maybe if I saw a photograph, I could nail down the time period.

"Hi, sweetie! What are you reading?" says my mom, appearing in the doorway out of thin air. Her reddish-brown wavy hair has glints of purple in the sickly fluorescent light. She looks warm in her black leather jacket.

I slap my diary shut and shove it under my covers.

"Nothing. Diary stuff. Private stuff."

"Are you writing about Bryce?"

I frown, thinking for a moment. It would be better to start rambling about crushing on my friend again rather than tell her I'm still trying to prove Akasha was real.

"Kat, what were you thinking, running off like that? You scared the hell out of me! What would Grandma say?

You're lucky that Bryce's mother did the right thing and called me after he called the police. Do you know I was at the police station getting ready to send an Amber Alert to the media?" says my mom. I say nothing.

"You can sit there like an angry mute. I don't care. I'm just glad you're safe now," she says, as a short gray-haired man appears in the doorway.

He's looking down at me, past the wire frames of his glasses. Then he looks down at the clipboard he's holding.

"Katelyn Medena, Mrs. Medena, my name is Dr. Werdiger. I'll be conducting your evaluation."

He's looking at me the same way my old school principal used to after I'd been sent to the office for day-dreaming in class.

This is not going to go well; I can feel it.

Chapter 3

"So, Katelyn, I see here you've had some excitement recently. Vancouver is a dangerous place for a minor, let alone a girl who's run away from her caregiver," says unhappy Dr. Werdiger. Faint musky cologne has followed him into my room.

"I'm her mother. Please, call me Becky," says Mom. She dusts her hands nervously and shoves a set of freshly manicured rose-pink nails towards the doctor. He shakes her hand cautiously.

"Becky it is. I'm the psychologist you were slated to meet with yesterday morning. It's unfortunate that we had to reschedule our appointment ... and change the venue." Dr. Unhappy sounds irritated. I wonder if Mom's biker-style jacket has made a bad impression. As though she heard me, she removes it and sits down.

"I'm so sorry about that. It was just a misunderstanding," says Mom. I am still saying nothing.

"In light of Katelyn's actions, her evaluation will determine whether we move forward with long-term admittance to BC Children's or take an out-patient approach." We must look terrified, because he quickly adds, "Don't worry; this isn't an incarceration. Provided we don't detect any serious cause for concern, from there we can admit her to a local group home and continue treatment in a more comfortable environment."

"Katelyn, say something."

"Something." I glare at my mother, refusing to address Dr. Unhappy directly.

"Being uncooperative is not going to help you through your evaluation."

"Fine, Dr. Werdiger, I'll cooperate. I don't know what else there is to say, though. Did Dr. MacDonald send my file?"

"Yes, we have his notes and his initial diagnosis."

"So, you know what *I* think. Now I just need to know what *you* think."

"It's not that simple, Katelyn, but if you help *us*, we will do our best to help *you*."

"Katelyn will cooperate. She wants to get better." Mom confidently folds her hands in her lap.

I grind my teeth silently, pushing my hair back and away from my face.

"I'll give you two some privacy." To me, Mom adds, "I'll bring you back a hot chocolate."

"Now then, Katelyn," Dr. Werdiger says as he takes a seat in the armchair next to the magazine-covered side table. He pushes his glasses back up the bridge of his nose. "Let's talk a little bit about why your mother brought you to Vancouver in the first place."

"Okay. I'm here because I told my mom that I think a girl from the past is talking to me." I manage to make my tone as matter-of-fact as possible. "I think I'm having this girl's dreams. And I think she's writing in my diary."

"And you believe this girl is you in a past life?" Dr. Werdiger is equally straightforward.

"I don't really know. I don't know why I told my mom all that stuff. I don't know where I got the idea. It just seemed to be the right thing when I found handwriting that didn't look like mine in my own diary — and because of the dreams."

"Your mom thinks you might be suffering from epileptic seizures, despite that diagnosis being ruled out some time ago. Your regular psychiatrist, Dr. MacDonald, isn't quite sure how these fantasies are helping you. Your mother also thinks you may be using drugs. She says you've come home smelling like marijuana on several occasions. She thinks you may have tried other drugs." Dr. Werdiger is obviously trying to read my face and gauge my reaction. I am a blank sheet with ice-cold eyes.

"I don't do drugs, not even pot. I'm from Nelson. I mean, I've come home smelling like pot. You can't get away from it. I don't think I have epilepsy, either. I don't want attention — from anyone. I have no idea why I'm dreaming and writing the things I am."

"I notice you're using present tense. These dreams and writings are still happening?"

I say nothing, but I know the look of "caught" is written on my face.

"Okay, let's talk a little bit about your father. You aren't in touch?"

"No, but that doesn't bother me. He left when I was a baby. Mom and I are perfectly fine on our own."

"But you're not fine; you're in the hospital. You ran away."

He's trying hard to rattle me. I can't allow it to work, but I don't know how to outsmart him. I have to keep my mouth shut.

"Well, it's apparent to me that you are not hallucinating or abusing a substance of some sort. So, I'm ready to refer you to a group home for ongoing counseling. The province doesn't have a suitable facility in Nelson. We can place you here in Vancouver or in Kelowna. It might be easier for your mother if you were closer to home."

"Do I have a choice?" I shift uncomfortably in my bed. I've been sitting too long and I'm suddenly aware of the awkward mismatch between my pajamas and his business-casual slacks and collared shirt.

"I'm not comfortable releasing you from this hospital if we can't agree on a treatment plan for you. If you hadn't run away from your mother, things might be different, but as it is … I'm afraid we're a bit stuck."

"I'd like to stay here in Vancouver." I leave out that I don't particularly want to make things easier for my mom. Something completely bizarre is happening to me and I need her support. Instead she's putting my brain under a microscope.

"Okay, let me make a few calls and see where we can find a bed for you. We might have you placed by tomorrow."

"Thanks." I am trying to be grateful and cheerful, but I know this is not what Dr. Werdiger sees as he leaves my room. I don't care what he thinks as long as I can stay in Vancouver. Being here is my only chance to find answers.

Mom comes back with her coffee and my hot chocolate. I take the cup and smile.

"I hope you don't mind, but I'm going to leave again in a bit. I called Patricia Lindstrom and I'm going to meet her for a late lunch."

"Say hi to Nanny Patty for me." I smile. Thinking of my former second mother lifts me slightly. "I just wish there was more for me to do here. I don't know anyone. I don't want to hang out in their teen lounge and I'm not supposed to wander around. But Dr. Werdiger says he can get me into a group home soon, maybe even tomorrow. I can handle a boring day and another night here." I am able to fake cheerfulness now. Staying in Vancouver is a good thing, even if I have to submit to mental health treatment.

"Why don't you call Bryce, sweetie? He's really broken up about calling the police. He did the right thing, but I think he feels like he betrayed you."

"He *did* betray me!"

"Katelyn, you have to understand the position you put him in."

"I know. This sucks. For everyone. I'm sorry. I don't know how many times I can say I'm sorry before it loses all meaning. But something is happening to me. I know I'm not crazy." I also know arguing with Mom isn't helpful. I take a deep breath. "But I know I'm not being haunted by a past life. I will work with Dr. Werdiger to figure out what's really going on. And I already texted Bryce. He's coming to see me later today."

"Thank you, sweetie. It's good to see you putting the pieces back together. That's all I'm asking for." Mom kisses my forehead, shrugs her jacket back on, and leaves again.

My phone jingles.

Are you decent? I'm down in the lobby.

Bryce! I jump up to the bathroom and start brushing my hair.

Chapter 4

I sit in the aggressively cheerful yellow-walled teen lounge with my diary and a copy of *FLARE* that is at least ten years old. I've finally brushed out my tangled jungle of hair and I feel more presentable to the civilized world. I told Bryce to meet me here instead of coming to my room. A new nurse came in, so I didn't miss my chance to scramble out of my PJs and be human for the first time in over a day.

I can't concentrate enough to write, so I flip through page after page of fashion photos. I don't know if I should see Bryce; part of me wants to stay angry, but the longer I wait to find out if I'm cool with him, the harder it will be for both of us to talk. I might have done the same thing if a runaway turned up at my house in the middle of the night.

I must look unapproachable because none of the other kids that come and go from the lounge venture a greeting or comment in my direction. After what feels like hours, I look up to see Bryce walk through the door.

In the brightly lit room, I get a better look at him than I had in his basement at night. He's grown taller again.

The minor case of acne he used to have is gone and his skin is smooth, the color of oak wood. His jet-black hair is a little different; his bangs are a bit longer and sculpted more carefully than before. His light brown eyes have an almost golden hue now.

"Hey runaway, how 'ya doin'?" asks Bryce playfully. This is his way of breaking the tension. I smile to show him I'm not planning to chew him out. I'm desperately curious where his parents are. His mother will be hovering somewhere nearby.

"Can't complain now that I've got such fine accommodation." I roll my eyes and survey the room.

"I wish you could have stayed at my house, but it just wasn't gonna work out."

"I know. I put you in a terrible position. It's all sorted now. I'm probably going to stay at a group home here in Van until they tell me I'm officially not crazy."

"You're not crazy. Nobody's saying that. Not even —" Bryce stops short of naming someone.

"Not even your father?"

"He doesn't think you're crazy. A bit weird for a twelve-year-old, but hey, aren't we all?"

"Yeah. Coming from an academic and music prodigy."

"This hospital thing is just something they have to do. You can't run away without them making a big deal out of it."

"True. And even if I get into that group home, I don't know how long I'll be there." I pause, think, and switch to sarcasm mode. "As long as it takes me to come up with a cover story for two styles of handwriting in my diary — not to mention Hindi — along with a believable reason for being delusional or a motivation for lying, whichever comes to me first."

Deep down I'm not joking. I reached out for help and Bryce slapped my hand. I know he had to, but I can't change how I feel. I shared a secret — with Bryce and Mom. And that trust led me to the Children's Hospital kids' lounge.

"Maybe we can hang out while you're here. I can show you around a bit." I want to take Bryce's olive branch. I can go for the occasional plate of fries without bringing him back into my circle of trust. Dr. MacDonald called it compartmentalization, which is when you separate feelings that don't go well together — so, you can ignore the part of you that's mad at a person when you want to be friends with that person.

"Sure, I'd like that. I could use a little tour. I don't know what part of the city I'll be in yet, but I don't want to get lost trying to find my way around." I also don't want to sound too eager to get back into Bryce's social calendar.

"Just think, when you come back to the coast for university one day, you'll already know your way around."

"Yeah, that totally makes it worthwhile being held against my will as a mental patient." I cringe at the way that came out. "I'm sorry. I know how that sounds. It's not your fault I'm here, it's mine." I'm practicing again for my psychiatric audience. In reality, I'm pretty sure it's Mom's fault.

"It's okay. Your mom reminded me that you've got something like epilepsy, but they haven't diagnosed it. That's harsh." Bryce looks at me with pure pity.

"I barely remember those old gap-out sessions. They're not really happening anymore. I don't know why she still thinks I've got some brain disorder." I know exactly why Mom is confused. If she could only believe me, life would be so much easier.

"Still, it's more than most of us have to deal with."

"I guess it's possible there's something to it." I look away to a poster of a skateboard park on the opposite wall. Bryce and I are running out of topics and I'm too worn out for small talk.

"How about a game of pool?" I gesture to the pool table nearby.

"I'll rack."

We play pool for another hour before Bryce's mother peeks her head through the doorway. Radhika and I have always gotten along, even though she's shy. I wonder how she'll feel if she finds out I think I was an Indian girl in a past life. She smiles weakly at me with her painted maroon lips, not entering the lounge as Bryce says goodbye.

MOM COMES BACK with A&W burgers for our dinner so I don't have to eat hospital food again. I manage to smile a bit and let go of my anger about not being believed and about being in psychiatric care. I know I haven't stopped being mad about it, but I am moving in the right direction. Once I can convince myself I'm happy and normal, I can convince everyone else. The hard part will be drawing out my treatment long enough for some field trips around the city — if I can figure out how to get breaks from the group home. Still, I need to be ready. I'll need to make time to re-read all of Akasha's diary entries to be sure I have not missed anything important.

Dr. Werdiger knocks on my door as Mom stuffs the last of our fast food evidence into the waste bin.

"Katelyn, I have some good news for you," says Dr. Werdiger.

"You've decided I'm not crazy and you're letting me go home?"

"Let's not use the word 'crazy' from now on. I do have your group home ready, though."

"That was fast! So, lay it on me."

"You will be staying at Arbutus House in Kitsilano. Have you heard of the neighborhood?"

"I think so. Is it near downtown?"

"Katelyn won't be making any trips into the down-town core," Mom promises the doctor. She frowns at me.

"This house isn't really near the city center anyway. It's south of English Bay and east of UBC. It's mostly university students and families. A very safe and beautiful part of Vancouver."

"Sounds good. Mom, we can go check out UBC. Maybe I'll get to go to school there someday."

Mom frowns again, but Dr. Werdiger looks indifferent to my attempts to talk about anything other than psychiatric care.

"It's good to have plans and goals. For now, let's worry about getting you better," says Dr. Werdiger.

I briefly consider that I wouldn't get into UBC anyway. Then I wonder if Dr. Werdiger doesn't think I would get in. Wouldn't he know better? Either way, he's right about one thing: first thing comes first. But his first thing and my first thing are different; I need proof of Akasha's life here.

"Here is the package on staying at Arbutus House. There's a resident's agreement — which your mother will need to sign — house rules, and a few brochures for activities in Kitsilano. You're due at the house to meet the on-site supervisor Mariah and your counselor, Jane. I'll be working with you and Jane once a week, but you'll need to see Jane every day to start. Tomorrow morning, the nurse on duty will come in around ten a.m. and help you check out. From there, you can head straight to Arbutus House. Do you have any questions?" Dr. Werdiger shifts his gaze to Mom.

"I think we have everything we need. I'll look over this package with Katelyn tonight."

"Excellent. Katelyn, next time I see you will be at Arbutus House. Have a great night, ladies." Dr. Werdiger leaves abruptly.

Mom spends a few moments looking through the papers, which is good, because I have zero interest in reading them.

"Mom, can we do one thing after we get out of here tomorrow?"

"Sure, sweetie, what did you want to do?"

"The reason I ran away was because I wanted to go see Gastown in the city. I knew you wouldn't take me. I know you don't believe me about my dreams and my diary, and that's fine, you're probably right. But if I can just go look around and get it out of my system, I'll be able to get my head in the game, so to speak, when it comes to this counselor stuff."

Mom looks up from the stack of paper and eyes me carefully. Her deadpan expression suggests nothing about what she might be thinking. Is she angry? Is she scared? Am I about to get yelled at or cried on?

"Okay, Kat, we'll go. But so help me God, if you put one foot out of place or I so much as get a twinge of a feeling that you're going to bolt, I'll clamp a lock on your ankle for the next decade. Got it?"

"Yes, Mom, I've got it. Thank you. This means a lot to me."

"Why didn't you just ask the first time?"

"Would you have taken me?"

"Now we'll never know."

Mom gathers the Arbutus House papers, puts a hand on my thigh and leans in to kiss my forehead.

"Goodnight, Kat. You'd better be here in the morning."

Chapter 5

The drive down to Gastown takes us through the roughest blocks of East Hastings Street. I haven't been back to Vancouver since I was eight years old. I can remember flashes — the aquarium, an urban mall, the view of the city from our hotel room. I have no memories of being a baby or toddler here. I've only ever seen the scary part of the city on television or in photos. On the street today I see people who look worn, broken, drained, and wrung-out. The people here are beyond poor and addicted, they've been totally crushed by life on the street. But I can't look away.

My rural mountain town, Nelson, doesn't have a lot of homeless people, mainly because the winters are cold and snowy and because there are few places to sleep in public without being bothered. I'd be more likely to stumble across some hippy tenting in a park than a junkie.

After we have passed the blocks of lumpy sleeping bags and overflowing shopping carts, Mom pulls over and parks in front of a greasy-spoon diner.

"I'm not sure where you want to start, but I looked

at a map on my phone. We can walk along Water Street until we get to the Waterfront SkyTrain Station. From there, we'll see how close we can get to the Port of Vancouver. That's a recognizable landmark," says Mom. Her awkward tone is humoring me. My gut instinct is to yell, to tell her I really did have dreams about a girl from the past, and that I'm not making it up.

"This is great, Mom. I'm sure being here in person will be different than my dreams and it'll be easier to move on." I don't believe one word coming out of my mouth.

We close our car doors and I look up and around at this unfamiliar neighborhood. I see my reflection in the diner window and realize I stick out here; I'm a doe-eyed kid in a plain T-shirt and jeans with no business wandering around the city. Across the street, a community garden is growing a mishmash of vegetables and flowers. Creeping vines weave through the fence, hiding most of the rows nearest the road. I glance both ways along the sidewalk, briefly considering another escape. I look over at Mom, her reddish wavy hair practically wild behind her steely blue eyes. Her frown busts me instantly.

"I'm not going anywhere. We'll walk around. I'll stick with you, I promise."

"You better believe you will. If there's a next time, I'll let them lock you up." Mom glares at me. She starts slowly down the street and I follow, for my own safety as much as obedience.

We come to a gap in the downtown towers and I can see the sun shining on blue-green mountains to the north. As we cross a few more streets north of Hastings, I can see giant iron arms painted orange. I decide they must be used for lifting shipping containers and must mark the Port of Vancouver. We are close after all. We come to a halt underneath an old-fashioned grandfather clock. The morning sun adds a nostalgic yellow hue to the historic atmosphere of bare brick buildings, cobblestone streets, and antique lampposts.

"Waterfront Station is on our left. A green space called Crab Park is to the right. Which one do you want to try first? The station might give us a view of the port." Mom examines her phone closely. I can see that a part of her wants to help and my heart softens.

"No, let's try Crab Park. I think we should go towards those giant orange metal arms."

"You mean the dock cranes? Those weren't around in the nineteen-hundreds. Aren't you looking for where your ship landed?"

"I'm sure you're right and that nothing is left of Vancouver from a hundred years ago. It'll help me to see that in person, from whatever angle we view it."

"Okay. We want one more street up and another block over." Mom looks up from her phone and points towards the edge of the line of metal arms.

Crab Park does not disappoint me: it gives a clear view of the Port of Vancouver and its bright orange cranes.

As we walk along the concrete paths, the only problem is that I'm not learning anything. I don't know anything new, about Akasha or her fate. I realize that I hadn't been honest with myself about my expectations of this urban waterfront. I really had expected to find something that would make sense of the images and urges I've been having these last few months. My energy weakens with each step I take.

"Well, what do you think, should we make our way over to Waterfront Station now?" There is a hint of urgency in Mom's voice; she really wants to get this over with soon.

"Just a second … there *is* something," I say as a matte tile mosaic catches my eye. At the heart of a concrete slab, a steamship made of white and gray tile floats rigidly in a sea of blue and pink ceramic chips. The sunset in the background looks warm; golden clouds behind a hot orange sun. The men wearing turbans stare accusingly at me with blank tile faces. A compass surrounds the ship, and around that, a square border with the words, "*The Komagata Maru*" repeated below the letters *N*, *S*, *E*, and *W*.

"This was her ship," I whisper.

"What?"

"My … girl, Akasha. This is the ship she came to Canada on!" The prospect of a real lead sends adrenaline through my veins.

"This is a commemorative mosaic. You can't possibly

recognize anything in the picture. It's practically abstract. Don't latch on to the first thing you see."

"Why don't you just let me have it? You're itching to get going, so why not just let me think I've found something?"

"I'm sorry, sweetie, I'm just trying to help. Write it down. You can do some research when we get you settled."

Mom doesn't believe me, but she's got a point. I pull my notepad out of my backpack and write down everything I can think of about the picture, even things I already knew.

Komagata Maru
— *Steamship*
— *India*
— *Port of Vancouver*

It's not enough. But it's something.

"Let's go. I'm not going to have some kind of psychic vision just standing around here."

Mom puts her arm around my shoulder and pulls me along as she turns back towards the car.

AFTER A DRIVE-THRU burger lunch just outside downtown, we reach Arbutus House around two o'clock. The yard is quiet. Apart from a small sign above the door, there is nothing special about the place. Mom knocks on the door. I can tell from the way she's fidgeting with her car keys that she's nervous. I feel the same way and I shift the weight of my backpack as we stand on the step. Mom knocks on the door again. We wait. Finally, a shadow moves behind the frosted glass pane next to the door.

"Good afternoon. May I help you?" A round woman shorter than Mom stands in front of us. She has long flowing black hair that is scraggly at the ends as though it hasn't been cut in years. Her brown skin is weathered. She wears only a bit of brown eye makeup. Lines and bags under her eyes give her a defeated look.

"I'm Becky Medena. This is my daughter Katelyn. We were told you'd be expecting us."

"Yes, come right in." The woman breaks into a warm smile and steps aside. "My name is Mariah. I'm the house manager."

"Dr. Werdiger mentioned you. Will we be meeting a counselor named Jane as well?"

"Not today. Jane doesn't live on site. She usually doesn't consult with parents until further into treatment."

I stand in the entryway awkwardly, unsure if I should enter the living room or head down the hall to the left to look for a bedroom. The kitchen is on our right, and unless the house has a basement, there isn't much room to move around.

"Katelyn, let me show you to your room. Mrs. Medena — sorry, Becky — would you like to wait in the living room for us? The other girls are all out this afternoon, so you'll have some lovely peace and quiet."

A wary feeling creeps up the back of my spine. I'm about to get a lecture Mom won't be hearing.

"Sure. I'll have a seat until you're sorted."

"Katelyn, please follow me. You're in the last bedroom on the right." Mariah marches down the hallway and I follow obediently.

The room has two twin beds with plaid bedspreads, two nightstands, and two wardrobes on the far wall. There is no sign of another occupant.

"You have the room to yourself for the time being. I wouldn't get used to it though. With summer starting, we're bound to see another new face soon." Mariah is pleasant, but not friendly. I set my backpack down on the bed next to the room's only window, claiming my spot.

"So ... is everyone here ... crazy?"

Mariah looks at me for a long moment.

"My dear, even if I wanted to try to answer you, that's not an appropriate question. Take a moment to put your things away and come back to living room." Mariah leaves abruptly. I was wrong about the lecture — clearly this woman is merely the gatekeeper, and hopefully a cook. My stomach rumbles with protest at the remnants of my greasy burger lunch.

I remove my clothes from my backpack and put them in the shelves on the bottom level of the wardrobe. I have nothing worth hanging. My diary gets the prime real estate inside my nightstand drawer. Once I have a room-mate, I might need to do a better job of hiding it, but I can't imagine Mariah will care in the slightest about my personal thoughts. I sit down on the bed to draw out my time alone.

My window looks out on the house's backyard. The yard has a picnic table, a garden, and an oak tree with a tire swing. Arbutus House is the perfect place to be a normal kid.

Too bad I'm the farthest thing from normal this house has ever seen.

Chapter 6

Mom doesn't stay long and thankfully Mariah *is* the resident cook. While she chops and scrapes and stirs in the kitchen, I slip back to my room to re-examine Akasha's entries one more time. I re-read each of her notes in turn. There is nothing new.

I pull a fresh pen out of my backpack and sit cross-legged on the end of the bed with my diary in front of me. I look over at the open door. Sounds of Mariah preparing dinner still carry down the hall. No one else is in the house.

I close my eyes and try to picture the girl from my dreams. I've seen her reflection, but the image was fleeting. Flowing wavy ebony hair and honey eyes met me briefly. Pink lips and an oval face with skin like warm toffee. I picture the brown sari I saw looking down with my own eyes as Akasha crawled up onto the old Vancouver pier.

A thick fog flows over me and my mind's eye grows dark. A light flickers in the distance, heading towards me, slowly opening up the scene around me.

I am seated at a writing desk in a finely appointed sitting room. My hands are brown again. The sleeves of my old-fashioned dress are navy-blue cotton with ivory lace trim at the cuffs. I am writing a letter.

Vancouver, September 10th, 1914

Laura, my friend, I can only pray that this letter reaches you some day. You may have learned that I stole away with Sanjay to come to Canada. Things went so terribly wrong. I was a stowaway in his trunk, our goal almost achieved. I was moments from being carried to freedom with my true love. God had other plans and I was cast overboard in an argument. I barely survived. The ship's passengers were detained at the port. Only a few were admitted. I did not see Sanjay among them.

My misery does not end there. I am being held by a man who said he ran a home for girls. I quickly discovered he is a liar, but it was too late. How could I have been so naive? I should have let myself starve on the street.

I do not believe I will ever find the money to return home. I'm not sure if I can even afford to post this letter. If he finds this sheet of paper, he will tear it up and I will feel the back of his hand on my cheek.

If you read these words, do whatever may be in your power to put this letter in Sanjay's hands. The Komagata Maru left Vancouver on July 23rd of this year. He may already be home as I write. I pray that he will come back to Canada, back to Vancouver. Whatever else you might do, please pray for me, and for my safety.

Your Loving Friend Always, Akasha

I fold up the letter and stuff it into a pocket in the skirt of my navy dress. I will not risk leaving home unescorted, but I must hide my letter. I may not get a chance to write unobserved again for a long time. Where to hide it? What spot can I trust to be both safe and secret?

I walk around the room anxiously. I need a hiding place and quickly. The porcelain flower vase? No, there are a lot of arguments in this house and the vase could get smashed. The underside of the sofa? No, not secure enough. Behind a painting? No, it could be moved or taken away. The fireplace? If I could find a loose brick, it might do until I have an opportunity to put it in the post. Is the grout old enough to crumble?

I test each outer brick around the fireplace. When I come to the top of mantle, one brick is slightly loose. I grab a letter opener from the writing desk and pry the brick out. I scrape frantically at the grout left behind. I make just enough room for my letter to fit comfortably before I replace the brick. I sweep the grout rubble and dust into the fireplace with the toe of my shoe.

"Akasha?" says a smooth, deep male voice from behind me. And blackness returns.

I OPEN MY eyes to find myself still sitting on my plaid bedspread in Arbutus House. No sounds come from the hallway. Only white noise knocks inside my ears. My heart thuds thick beats that prickle with primal fear. I had been Akasha again. I can feel her terror still gripping me. She was so afraid of being discovered.

I look down at my diary. There is fresh writing on the page, but it doesn't look like mine. It looks like hers: Akasha's. The text starts with "Vancouver, September 10, 1914 … Laura, my friend."

It worked! I wrote her words again! It's all in English to someone named Laura. Who is Laura? Does it matter?

"Girls! Dinner's ready!" Mariah calls from the kitchen.

A blond girl pops her head around my doorjamb.

"Hey, new girl. Stop writing for a minute and come get some food."

The blonde is gone again in a beat.

How can I eat dinner now? How will I get to sleep tonight?

No matter how I sleep tonight, I have something to do tomorrow. I have a fresh lead. And I now know for sure that I was right about the *Komagata Maru*. Suck it, Mom! Ha!

My next goal is to get more information about the house Akasha stayed in. If I'm lucky, it's still standing — with the original fireplace intact.

SLEEP DOESN'T COME easily after my outrageously successful writing session. But I finally drift off. I slowly blink awake, but I know I'm dreaming.

I am sitting in my favorite place in the whole world. The morning sun adds a sprinkling of tiny glass gems to the basin of water lilies in front of me. The square stone tiles on the ground have fresh green grass growing in place of grout. My stone bench has enough room for one other occupant. I am waiting for Sanjay. My heart is full of anticipation and love. A cool breeze kisses my cheek.

I am supposed to be meditating, practicing to clear my mind of thoughts. I had chosen a plain piece of linen to focus on. But how can I turn away the image of Sanjay's face or the promise of rugged Canadian forests?

After serving our simple breakfast of dal and naan, I ate my own portion and cleaned basin after basin of dishes. After my meditation time is over, I will scrub the floor in the main hall. I should want nothing more than to serve at the temple. I am a failure as a devotee.

Guru Nanak, please send me enough strength to say no if Sanjay asks me to go to Canada with him. I will work hard on meditating properly. I will come here, stare at the lilies, and devote myself only to God. But first, I must have the strength to listen to my head and not my heart.

"Akasha," whispers a voice in my ear. Sanjay is so quiet that I almost believe the word is still a mere thought.

I open my eyes and his square jaw and chiseled facial features clash with his giddy smile. Sanjay stands tall and confident before me, his bright eyes full of excitement.

"I hoped you would not come today." I avert my eyes to the ground.

"Why not? Do you not love me?" Sanjay's voice has a hint of panic.

"I will not lie. I love you still." I take a deep breath to muster my courage. "But you must leave here and never return."

"Nonsense. You must come with me." Sanjay kneels on the ground in front of me.

"Your father would have me burned."

"Father will never know. We leave for Canada next week. Agree to be my wife and I will smuggle you out in one of my trunks. I have spoken with a man who has done such a thing and he told me what to do." Sanjay is looking at me intently and I risk making eye contact. He is so persuasive. I sit up straight to strengthen my resolve.

"So what if we make it to Canada? Your father will never allow you to break your engagement. He will stand at your side until you are married. Now that you have told him you want a love match instead, he will be all the more determined to see you married as he wishes."

"If my mother still lived, she would soften his heart. Father has lost his compassion and his humility. He has become obsessed with the singular notion that our family must become Canadian." Sanjay takes my hands in his.

"Suppose your plan works and we make it into Canada and run away from your father. How will we live? We will not be citizens. We will have no money and nowhere to go." I can feel fear quickening my pulse as I look around the garden for witnesses.

"You are wrong again." Sanjay grins. "I have written to my friend Pameer asking for help. He lives in Vancouver and can shelter us. His answer finally arrived!" Sanjay removes a folded piece of paper from his pocket and holds it out like a medal.

I look up again to meet Sanjay's gaze. His energy is contagious. I allow the picture of our Canadian home back into my mind. My heart has won the battle.

"All right, Sanjay. I will try. I will go with you and pray for our success."

Sanjay squeezes my hands.

"You will not be sorry, my love. We have a long and difficult path ahead, but all will be worth it when we marry."

The sound of footfalls on the stone path behind me startles both of us and Sanjay drops my hands.

"Good day, Miss," says Sanjay as he nods in farewell.

My heart surges with a mix of anxiety and happiness as he leaves.

The footfalls behind me grow louder and closer. I close my eyes to discourage the passerby from engaging me in conversation.

"Akasha," says a stern deep voice. I open my eyes again to see Sanjay's father standing before me, taller than Sanjay with a full beard and skin weathered by time. His dark eyes bear me no affection, only rage.

"I heard Sanjay's voice here a moment ago. I take it you have not discouraged him as you should have done."

"Sir, I have told him to go and do as you instruct." Fear grips my chest as Mr. Hasan glares at me.

"You are a liar. Shiva will punish you accordingly. We

are a Hindu family and my son will wed a Hindu bride, not a Sikh. Your attempt to ingratiate yourself to my household by adding Hindi to your linguistic skills was pointless. Do not worsen your fate by tempting my son any further. We are leaving for Canada in one week. If you cause him to disobey me, if you so much as write him a letter once we have gone, you will find me to be a ruthless enemy. My brothers will come to this place, take you, and sell you to a whorehouse in Agra. A year after that, they will come for you again and burn you in the street, you filthy orphan!" Mr. Hasan's eyes blaze with hatred.

"I have not and will not convince Sanjay to do anything he does not wish to." I am angry and terrified. Tears well in my eyes and sobs tug at my throat.

"I have nothing more to say to you." I open my mouth to defend myself again, but Mr. Hasan is already walking away.

I hold my breath until his footfalls are gone again. And then I press my hands up to my face to contain the weeping. I rock back and forth on the bench until I regain control.

I WAKE UP in a strange, dark room, terror pounding the air out of my lungs. I look over at the alarm clock. It is five-twenty in the morning. I am in Arbutus House. I am Katelyn.

Chapter 7

*T*here are three other girls here at Arbutus House. All are older than me and have been here for quite a while. They are: Yolanda, a fellow runaway; Therese, a former underage prostitute; and Melody, a schizophrenic who just got out of the hospital and is here trying to adjust to the outside world again. Melody is the only girl who gets a room to herself, apart from my temporary good luck.

My roommates are all normal-looking girls. Melody is tall with an auburn braid. Therese has creamy white skin and very pale platinum hair with brown roots. Yolanda is fairly heavy set with a freckled face that makes her look happy in spite of whatever compelled her to run away from home.

They are all pleasant and bright enough, although none feels like a friend yet. You would never know that my housemates were confined for mental health treatment. It has been an uneventful week.

I had to wait these seven days before Mariah and Jane would let me have a visitor. I've been texting back and forth with Bryce, but on Jane's advice, I invited Mom to be my first guest. I'm waiting for her in the living room, looking out the window for her green sedan. Checking the mirror on the far wall, my jean shorts and T-shirt look like any other summer outfit. My long wavy hair is clean and brushed. Nervous energy darts between my wide eyes and my lips are pressed into a firm line. Mariah sent the other girls to the community center so I'll have privacy to talk with Mom. I'm eager to tell her all about my talks with Jane.

I've made progress. I've discovered that I have feelings of resentment about my father leaving Mom and me and having no presence in my life after I was six months old. I know that Akasha's writing is really my own, distorted in an attempt to draw attention from authority figures apart from my mom. My dreams are a manifestation of a desire to be special, intensified by my fascination with both India and Edwardian culture. I stopped short of confessing to smoking pot; I will not be able to produce a credible account in the event anyone who actually has smoked it hears me. Where did Mom get the idea someone would give a twelve-year-old girl a joint? I mean, even in Nelson, that's a bit much.

So, I have carefully crafted my cover story. Jane believes me. If I can convince Mom too, and get her to sign a form, I may receive precious day-pass privileges. As a minor, I will require an escort, but I can be excused from Arbutus House for outings of my own choosing. I've got my fingers crossed Bryce's big brother Mitchell will be up for it. Otherwise I'll be stuck with Mom and my old nanny. Until now, I have only left the house for brief group outings to coffee shops and parks.

Mom's green sedan finally rolls into view and comes to a stop alongside the sidewalk. She isn't alone. A head of pixie-short, straw-blond hair sits in the passenger side next to Mom's ruddy curls and black leather jacket. Patricia, or to me, Nanny Patty, has come along. Mom mentioned that she had moved from her motel onto Patty's couch, so it's no shock to see them together. She's one of few people Mom knows in Vancouver.

"Hey, Mariah. My mom is here, but she brought a friend. Is it okay for both of them to be here?" I call back towards the kitchen. Mariah emerges, wiping her hands on a tea towel. Her long black hair is swept up into a messy bun on her head. She is wearing an apron that really doesn't work with her stocky frame.

"Do you know the other person?" asks Mariah.

"It's my old nanny. Well, she's not old, it was just a long time ago that she was my nanny," I say. I can hear the nerves in my voice.

"That's fine; I'm sure it's not a problem. But until you get a chance to talk it over with Jane, keep the conversation light. If it gets too emotional, you'll have to ask your nanny to wait in the car," says Mariah. She has a worried look on her face.

A knock on the door interrupts us and I give a small jump. Where is this anxiety coming from? Maybe I really do have a screw loose if I can't keep cool around Mom. Mariah gestures and I open the door.

"Good morning, sweetie!" says Mom, beaming. Patty stands behind her, wearing a small smile and the weathered denim jacket from my childhood. She is not as tall as I remember her, but still lean and strong.

"Hi, Mom. Hi, Nanny Patty." I'm looking at Patty as I hug my mom.

"Hi, Katelyn, it's good to see you. You don't have to add the 'nanny' part anymore," says Patty. She smiles, showing off the lines in her cheeks framing uneven teeth and a pointed chin.

"Well, then, you can call me Kat. Mom does. I can't believe you've still got that jacket. You look exactly how I remember you."

"Wow, I'll take that as a compliment."

"Aren't you going to invite your guests in?" says Mariah from behind me.

"Yes, please come in." I step aside and sweep my arm inward as a welcome.

Mom and Patty step inside and put their shoes on the plastic mat. They follow me to Arbutus House's simple living room. A pastoral painting hangs over the single couch facing the bay window. Patty sits in an armchair while Mom and I take opposite ends of the couch.

"How have you been? Is everything going all right? Are you making progress?" says Mom.

"I'm not supposed to talk much about therapy, but

it's going well. Lots of progress. Jane can't be here today, but she's going to call you later and give you an update."

"Well, what would you like to talk about?" Mom wrings her hands, looking around as though she might be on camera. She fluffs the wavy layers of her hair and pulls out a tube of gloss to refresh the thin red sheen on her lips.

"Tell me what you've been up to this week. It's been pretty quiet for me here."

"I've been staying with Patty. Just taking it easy, trying not to spend too much money. The shopping here is amazing!" says Mom.

"Your mom has been exploring the Mount Pleasant neighborhood while I'm at work," says Patty. Her voice sounds scratchy, as though overused for a long time.

"I heard you became a social worker. What's that like?" I'm genuinely curious and I'd love to talk about something that has nothing to do with my situation.

"Kat, she doesn't want to talk about that. Not here and now," says Mom. She looks around again.

"My work would probably bring you down. You don't need that right now," says Patty.

"Let's make a plan for an outing. What would you like to do, Kat? When they say you can go out, that is," says Mom.

"I don't know. You have to sign a form so I can get passes to leave the house without a staff member. But after that, we could do anything. I still haven't seen much of Vancouver, so I don't know what I'd be into around here."

"Think about it and do some research. I'll talk with Jane and I'm sure we can arrange for a nice afternoon together," says Mom. She sounds irritated. It's the tell-tale sign that she's losing patience with something I've done. The upside of being at Arbutus House is that I won't get a talking-to from Mom at the end of the day. I'm sure she's got lots of talking points saved for the drive back to Nelson.

"I'll put some thought into it too. I think it should be just the two of you, but I'd be happy to make some suggestions," says Patty.

"All right, then. We won't keep you much longer. I know we're not supposed to be here all afternoon," says Mom as she stands up. She looks uncomfortable. I can't tell if Arbutus House is making her nervous or if it's because of all her stored-up anger at me.

"Text me when you've talked to Jane," I say as Mom gives me a short squeeze. We exchange cheek kisses. Patty gives me a quick hug. Mom gives me a lingering smile. "I'm sorry if I seem a bit weird, sweetie. It's just that I didn't think we'd be … here." Mom gestures at the walls. "I mean, in Vancouver longer than a second opinion. It's okay, though."

Minutes later, I am back at the living room window waving goodbye. I had expected our visit to be longer. Mom's frustration at being stuck in Vancouver has caught me off guard. I feel like something bad has happened that I can't quite remember — like I'm waking from a nightmare that has already started to fade. A flash of anger pulses through me. *How dare you? It's okay? It's your fault we're stuck here, Mom!* Then again, it was me who ran from her in Surrey. Compartmentalization. I need to keep my cool at Arbutus House. I can always hash it out with Mom on the drive home.

I RETURN TO my room to read. Our television hours are strictly rationed and the only TV in the house is in the living room, as well as the shared computer. I will be delighted when I receive computer time, although supervised, hopefully along with my day passes. I read with the door open, not just for personal preference; I'm making a statement to Mariah that I have nothing to hide.

An unexpected knock startles me. I look up from my book to see Mariah standing in the doorway with a wiry, greasy girl with blotchy skin who looks to be a couple of years older than me.

"Katelyn, I'd like you to meet your new roommate. This is Rayanne," says Mariah. The girl stares at the floor, and then looks past me out the window to the backyard.

"Uh, hi, Rayanne," I say. I am filled with dread. Part of me hoped the other bed would stay crisp, clean, and unoccupied. I have never shared a room with a stranger before. The experience will not be made more bearable by a girl who looks ready to scratch her own arms off.

"I'll leave you two to get acquainted," says Mariah.

"So … what are you in for?" I'm joking, but the unease in my voice is hard to hide.

Rayanne whips her head towards me and spits her response. "It's not funny, my being here."

"Sorry. I didn't think it was. I'm just making conversation." My arms are raised in surrender.

"I'm drying out. Meth. It was this or stay in the hospital." Rayanne sets her bag down on the empty bed. She remains standing, awkward and angry.

"If it makes you feel any better, I'm crazy. Dissociative Identity Disorder, among other things. And I'm a runaway. My mom thinks that's the worst thing a kid can do." I try to sound nonchalant as I carefully scrape to the side of my mind my curiosity about whether Rayanne should be in a drug-specific home for youth.

"Nothing's worse than withdrawal!" Rayanne glares at me. I take a moment to evaluate her eyes. Raw hunger for something I've never tasted is consuming the girl.

"I wish there was something I could do for you."

"You can't help me. Nobody can help me."

"We could try to get along. While we're stuck together, at least."

"I won't be good company for a few days, maybe longer. Sorry, but that's the way it is."

"Can't they give you something for the symptoms?"

"They already have. It doesn't work."

"If you smoke, cigarettes, I mean, I think you have to leave the property. Unless you're nineteen. You're not nineteen, are you?"

"No, but they're going to let me smoke. I don't care."

"Why don't I give you some time in here by yourself? You can put your stuff away, get changed, and settle in."

"You're not afraid I'll steal your stuff?" A hint of a smile crosses Rayanne's face. It's gone again in a moment.

"Unless you want some old clothes and some crappy makeup, there's nothing to steal." My mind's eye flashes to my diary in the nightstand. I'll need to move it under my mattress when Rayanne's asleep tonight. As obvious as under my mattress is, it's at least slightly more secure than my nightstand drawer. I want anyone who goes after my diary to have the dirty feeling of digging it out from under my mattress before they get access to my secrets. I pause for a long moment, torn as to whether I should rescue my diary immediately — revealing both its existence and hiding spot — or risk leaving it alone with Rayanne. I turn and walk out empty-handed, giving Rayanne a forced smile as I leave.

Chapter 8

The other girls are still gone and the living room is too quiet. I am not allowed to turn on the television, which seems to be an unfair rule in a house I am also not allowed to leave alone. I want my day passes, so I obey all the rules.

I would look for company in the kitchen, where Mariah is still baking, but I know she will put me to work. So I go out to the backyard rather than getting roped into the next batch of whatever she's making.

I sit on the tire swing and nudge the ground with my toe to start a soothing sway. My brown canvas shoes are covered in faded pen-ink doodles, childish enough to be embarrassing while comfortable enough to still be my favorite shoes. I feel like someone is watching me. I am careful to keep my eyes on the garden at the back of the property so I don't accidentally make eye contact with anyone who pops back into the house.

The garden reminds me of home, of summers with Mom, and further back, with Patty. My memories of Patty are faint; I know her better from summer vacations when we came to the Coast or when she travelled to Nelson. Seeing her again under these circumstances isn't how I would have planned our reunion, but it was good to see her. I'm certain that if Mom and I had stayed here in the lower mainland, Patty would have been a big part of my life.

When Mom moved us to Nelson, I was four and a half. At first, I'd thought we were going on a big trip to have a grand adventure. I remember being so angry when I realized we weren't going back to Vancouver. I had made up my mind to hate Nelson and our house and everything about our new life. And then I met the boy who lived two doors down from me. We were friends almost immediately.

Bryce had a bicycle, albeit with training wheels. I'd never had as much as a tricycle. Mom and I had lived in a small apartment and she didn't want the clutter. But in Nelson, our home had three bedrooms and two floors. The only worry for Mom was the steep slope of the hill leading into the city center. We made a deal that, if I only rode my bike on the horizontal stretch of our block, I could get one. Bryce promised my mom that he would teach me and make sure I stayed on our block. I remember the story because Mom told it so often in the years afterwards. She had thought it was so cute that Bryce wanted to be my protector and teacher. My friendship with Bryce had that guardian-and-ward dynamic, even as we grew into the boys-and-girls-don't-mix years, and even when I came to resent the idea of a boy looking out for me. With high school on the horizon — and my crush on Bryce not successfully squashed — I wonder if our friendship was doomed even before he moved to Vancouver.

I look up at the house, wishing I had ignored Jane and invited Bryce to be my first visitor instead of Mom. But it's Rayanne's tired, pimple-spotted frown I see in the window. She beckons at me furiously and shouts that Jane is calling for me, so I hop off the tire and head inside.

I AM BACK in Jane's office, which is really just a converted garage at the far end of Arbutus House. She is running late, so I have time to re-read the motivational posters around the room. They feature sayings like, "SUCCESS Is A Journey, Not A Destination," and "CHALLENGES: Always Set The Trail, Never Follow The Path." The more I read them, the less they mean. I understand we are supposed to feel inspired and think positive thoughts. I think about the meaning of each poster, and then I think about motivational posters in general. I decide they are nonsense. I won't tell Jane this conclusion; if she put them up on her walls, I'm sure she likes them.

"Sorry I'm late, Katelyn. I know today is an important milestone for you, so I'm sure you're raring to go," says Jane as she sweeps into the room, flustered.

"That's okay. I've got nowhere else to be," I say as

sincerely and cheerfully as I can. I twist my hair back, ready to pay attention.

"Still, it's important to be on time. It's how we tell others we value them." I want to sarcastically ask her why she doesn't value me. I leave that comment mentally filed with the verdict on her posters.

"So, I saw my mom this morning."

"And how did that go?"

"She brought my former nanny, Patricia. I called her Nanny Patty, just like I was still four years old." I wonder if Jane will chastise me for having two visitors.

"How did it feel, seeing your mom and your nanny?"

"Great. I was kind of worried Mom was still mad about me taking off on her in Surrey, but I think she was more uncomfortable than anything else. It's weird that I'm here; we were just coming to Vancouver for an evaluation, not an extended stay."

"But how did *you* feel when you spoke with your mom?"

"I feel like ... I can remember a time when I wasn't worried so much. It was nice seeing my nanny too. It made me think about being a kid. I remembered when I moved to Nelson and I met my best friend. He's not really my best friend anymore. You can't have a boy for a best friend at my age." I say the words as though they're common knowledge.

"Why would you think you can't have a friend that's a boy?"

"It's complicated." I will not be telling Jane I developed a crush on my best friend. The deeper I bury that information, the less real it is. "And besides, his family moved to Vancouver, so that sort of put a stop to us really knowing each other. His parents don't really like him hanging out on social media too much. Or online at all for anything other than schoolwork."

"Hmmmm. It's hard to lose a friend." Jane looks down at her clipboard and flips up the top page. "Bryce is the boy whose house you went to when you slipped away from your mom. Had you asked your mom if you could visit while you were in Vancouver?"

"Yeah, I didn't run just to see Bryce. I wanted to see …"

"See what?"

"Isn't it there on your clipboard?"

"I'd like to hear your words."

"I wanted to see if I could find any evidence that proved Akasha, my past life, was real. If I found something that proved she'd been here, then Mom would have to listen to me, right?"

"Would you say you feel strongly about your dreams and writing about Akasha?"

"Yes, but that's not the point. What I was saying was —" I stop short of clarifying for Jane that it is Akasha's distinct writing in my diary, not my speculating about a dream, that drove my search for proof of a turn-of-the-century stowaway. Arguing isn't going to get me any day passes. I might even be asked to hand over my diary. I need to strike a balance; stay at Arbutus House, but get some slack in the leash and access to the city center.

"What I meant was that I understand it's all in my head. I was going through a rough patch, not just being lonely, but freaked out about high school coming in the fall. I honestly can't tell you why I got as worked up as I did."

Jane nods thoughtfully and makes notes on the top sheet of her clipboard.

"Well, Katelyn, I think we're ready to set you up with your day passes," she says. I am tingling with excitement. Precious freedom!

"That's awesome! I mean, I know I need an escort, but it's great to know I'm moving in the right direction."

"I think you are making progress, but let's not get carried away. Your mother still feels there may be a neurological issue involved in your case and we may yet pursue more testing. I want you to take it easy." Jane searches for something buried under a few pages on her clipboard. Is she reconsidering? Second-guessing my trustworthiness? Her attention returns to my face. Jane smiles at me.

"The way passes work here at Arbutus House is that you get three day passes per week. You can turn a pass in with Mariah and you've got six hours of free time outside the house. To be allowed out on your own, you need to be at least fifteen years old, so in your case, yes, you require an escort. It will need to be someone vetted by myself or Mariah in advance of your outing. I'm assuming your escort will be your mom, or possibly your nanny."

"My friend Bryce has a brother who's sixteen. Does that count?"

Jane frowned. "That wouldn't be *our* preference, but it would be up to your mother. She'd need to consent on paper."

"She will; she loves Bryce and his family. Mitchell, that's his brother, is really responsible." It sounds less convincing out loud than it had in my head.

"We'll make sure it all checks out. But regardless of who you go with, remember what I said about being on time. Wherever you go, make sure you've got time to get home before your pass expires. If you're late home once, we confiscate a pass. Twice, two passes. Three times late means we pull you back to supervised house outings only. Does that all make sense?"

"I've got it, loud and clear." I don't need to go far to feel free at the moment. I know six hours will become an unbearably small window once I get used to freedom again. Now, though, six hours of unrestricted roaming seems like bliss.

I WAKE UP the next morning to the sound of "Born to Be Wild" crooning from my phone. Bryce! I reach for the phone and pause mid-air. My diary! MY DIARY! Why is it out? *Did that sketchy Rayanne girl touch my stuff?*

I look over at her bed. It is empty and crudely made. Could it have been her? I can't think straight. Panic surges through me, clouding everything.

Okay, I need to calm down. My diary is still here. The worst case scenario is that Rayanne read it. Well, worse than that would be tearing pages out, but that's highly unlikely. I grab the book and stuff it under my mattress. I don't want it to see the light of day until I know what to do.

I check my phone. Bryce wants to hang out next week. Fine, that can wait. I pace slowly at the end of my bed, holding my phone. I look back at my diary. *What if Akasha wrote in it again?*

The idea that a new message is waiting excites me. I plunge my hand under the mattress and flip to the section of empty pages towards the back.

I now know I am in real danger. Sanjay is never coming for me. He has mourned me as lost. Or he has returned to India, married there, or left again for unknown shores. I will never know. Even if I find a way to mail my letter to Laura, it will make no difference. This man is evil. He will simply kill me if he thinks I am trying to escape.

He took me for a walk in the woods. He offered to show me the splendor that is the coastal rainforest in British Columbia. We walked along a trail not far from the city. It did not take long for him to drop hints that his girls stay with him until he decides to release them. None of the other girls are much older than I am. What causes him to release them, I have no earthly notion.

At the end of the trail, we reached a viewpoint of the ocean. How beautiful it was! I could not watch the surf crash into the rocks below without feeling fear. Then he softly mentioned how a girl had died at this point last year in an accident. He said no more, nor did he need to. I fully understood his meaning.

Reading Akasha's latest confession leaves me chilled and covered in goose bumps. I admit to myself what I've pretty much known all along. Akasha wants me to help find her killer and bring justice to her memory. But how can I possibly do that?

Chapter 9

A cool morning breeze sends ginkgo leaves fluttering in the tree behind the sidewalk where I'm waiting for Patty. I have my laminated day pass card in my hand, with one circle punched out of the first segment. I'm trying not to sweat too much on the card. I had not expected Jane's system to be so literal. Since each girl is granted a different number of outings per week, we are on the honor system with these little cards. I'll soon find it hard to forget that I'm allowed only three outings. But today, I am grateful. Patty has the day off and offered to take me downtown. Mom is catching up on work, so it will be me and Patty on our own, just like old times. Only now I'm chasing down a past life. I'm unsure what Patty will think about my current dilemma. Mom will have told her everything, with an eye towards some sort of neurological or psychological disorder.

I'm not sure if being outside by myself — technically off Arbutus House property — is some kind of violation, but I asked Mariah if I could wait outside and she said it was fine. After a week of living in what feels like a halfway house, I enjoy little moments of normality; having a shower, watching television, standing outside under a tree. I notice these moments now as they are some of the only reminders that I am not insane or a criminal, instead simply a mixed-up kid with one really big unofficial homework assignment.

Patty is taking me to the Central Library, Greater Vancouver's iconic downtown branch. Sure, there's a library here in Kitsilano, but I want the heart of the city for several reasons.

I believe the downtown branch will have historical documents, possibly records of immigrants coming into Canada, which are not found online. Even if they are online, I don't want to risk Mariah or Jane catching me doing research on "unhealthy" topics on the Arbutus House computer. Also, I might achieve a new level of connection with Akasha if I can touch something she touched. The letter will be out of my reach for now, possibly forever.

In addition to hard-copy documents, I want the history of Vancouver underneath my feet. It would be great to find my way back to Gastown, but even if I can't, I hope to find remnants of old Vancouver throughout the downtown core.

I don't know how long my time at Arbutus House will last. I have to assume that my fine line between being well-behaved enough for day passes, and yet still needing counseling, may backfire and stray over to a "healthy" seal of approval that will send me back to Nelson. So, every outing has to count.

Patty's car finally rounds the corner ahead and she comes to a stop in front of me.

"Hi, Katelyn! Hop in!" Patty is beaming with sparkling eyes that are wide enough to accentuate the lines around them. She is too excited to see a girl who should still be in trouble with her caregivers. "Still keen to see the library?"

"You bet! I've seen it in pictures, but I don't think I've ever been there in person." I won't tell Patty exactly what I'm looking for until I've had the duration of the car ride to evaluate her motives for helping me. If she's trying to catch me obsessing about "nonsense" so she can report back to Mom, I need to find a way to shake her once we get to the library.

"That is a great start to your time in Vancouver. Did you know the downtown branch of the Greater Vancouver Library has been used in many film and television settings?" Patty is driving slowly through the streets of Kitsilano, meandering through side streets too narrow for more than a single lane of traffic.

"I've heard that. I hope it's big. And modern! I love huge city buildings. We have nothing like that in Nelson."

"Well then, you're in for a treat!" Patty turns onto the Granville Street Bridge. We roll forward on the smooth asphalt until the towers of downtown Vancouver blot out the sun overhead. I can see how little of original Vancouver remains in the world of glass and concrete that exists today.

Patty reaches the library and we circle the block and arrive on the corner of Georgia and Hamilton.

"Oooooh, this never happens! Street parking!" Patty hits the breaks and swoops into a spot next to the sidewalk. I look up at the giant spiral building I've come to hang my hopes on. On the house computer, I learned that I can access historical photographs if I can find the Special Collections desk on level seven. Compared to the library in Nelson, a building with at least seven levels is bound to be a daunting place.

"You don't have to come in with me if you don't want to." I open my door as Patty fishes through her purse.

"Katelyn, your mother would skin me alive if I let you go off by yourself in downtown Vancouver." She pulls her phone out and swipes it open, tapping away as she looks between the screen and the parking meter next to us.

"I'll only be inside the library."

"Are you trying to get rid of me?"

"No, I just don't want to bore you. I wanted to wander around a library. That can't be very exciting for most people."

"I'm not most people. Besides, I'm sure you'll need help finding whatever you're looking for." I can tell from the playfully cheeky tone of Patty's voice that she knows exactly what I'm doing. But if she plans on helping me, I'm not going to slap her hand.

"I need to find the Special Collections desk. It's supposed to be on the seventh floor."

"Then let's go find a directory for this place so we can figure out how to get there."

Patty leads me around the corner and we follow the curve of the building to an opening in the concrete spiral. Once we're inside, huge glass walls showcase row upon row of books. It's the most impressive thing I've ever seen. I follow Patty through the main entrance, straight to a poster board with a map and the contents of each floor.

"We're already on level two. Looks like we can take the escalators all the way up. Come on," says Patty as she rushes off towards the core of the building.

"I'm not sure if I should mention this, but Mom isn't really keen on me doing the research I want to do here." As the metal stairs move upward, I feel like I'm leaving my stomach behind.

"I know that. Your mom is worried about you and I respect that. But she's always hung on a little tighter than she needs to. I know you're a responsible girl and I think a little harmless infatuation with the supernatural isn't going to kill you."

"So, you know everything." My gut churns even though my head tells me I'm all right. We transfer to the next escalator.

"I know you think you've had dreams about a past life and you wrote as much in your diary. Kids your age are already getting up to a lot worse, I can tell you. I told Becky that, but she's still worked up."

"I'm too weird to get into trouble like most kids."

"You're not weird, you're eccentric. And even if you were weird, it's better than having no imagination." We transfer again.

Patty examines her phone while I look up and around. We transfer again and again until we're on the top floor of the library. The city peeks in through the windows at the end of the hall and a rush of energy courses through me. We are in the heart of the biggest and best library I could hope to find.

"Excuse me," Patty says as she leans onto the Special Collections desk ahead. A middle-aged man is sitting at a computer behind the counter staring intently at his monitor. He finishes typing and rises to assist us. The tired eyes behind his wire-framed glasses are not happy.

"I'm sorry to bother you, but I'm hoping you can help us. My niece is working on a summer school project about ... what was it again, Katelyn?"

"Um, it's about a steamship called the *Komagata Maru*." I am a tightly wound ball of elastic nerves.

"Ah, yes." The librarian looks down at me over the top of his glasses. "The ship from Japan with Indian immigrants that got rejected coming into Canada." The librarian looked more interested in helping us. "I'm familiar with the *Komagata Maru*."

"My project is about a stowaway. All fictional, but I'd like to root it in real history. Can you help me find photographs? Or maybe the passenger list? I'm also interested in tracking what happened to the few people who made it into Canada." I grip the counter, looking over to Patty. She nods her encouragement.

The librarian hums as he thinks. "The first place I can direct you to is Simon Fraser University's historical website, but I'm sure you've found that already."

I nod, not willing to tell him that my internet time has been heavily monitored and I haven't risked looking up this information. I'd been reluctant to research the library system itself.

"I *did* come across it, but could you write the URL down for me, just in case I have trouble finding it again." He reaches for a piece of paper and loads the site on his screen.

"If you've looked at the site, you'll know that there isn't really a definitive passenger manifest. The documents we have conflict with each other, and we know many original records were lost."

"But do you have any documents?"

"By 'we,' I meant the royal sense. The documents are housed in a collection at the university."

I sigh. Patty puts her hand on my shoulder, waiting patiently.

"Can you show me any pictures of downtown Vancouver during the same period? As close as possible?"

"Sure. Would you like any hard copies?"

"You'll let me have the photos?" I can hear the excitement in the squeaky high volume of my voice.

"No, not the originals. I'll photocopy or print for you
at ten cents per page."

"Can I touch the photos?" The librarian frowns at
me. Even Patty looks a little concerned and I know I'm
pushing my luck.

"We prefer that you don't. And most of what I'll print
comes directly from our digital archive." The librarian
eyes me carefully.

Patty waits with me as he copies and prints photos of
old Vancouver.

"Well, that was better than nothing, right?" Patty's
voice is high as she touches my arm.

"Sure, it's a start." I can't hide my disappointment,
even though I knew I wouldn't just walk into a library
and find a photo of Akasha, complete with a date or
some kind of identification.

"Can I look at the computer before we go? There's
always someone standing over my shoulder at Arbutus
House. I don't know if I'll get in trouble for looking this
stuff up, but I get the impression they'd rather I forget
about all of this."

"Sure, we've still got time."

We stop at a bank of computers adjacent to the

escalators. On the top level, most terminals are empty. Patty sits in an armchair and resumes examining her phone while I click away.

I type in the *Komagata Maru* URL the librarian provided. I scroll through pages and photos. The grainy old pictures look nothing like the images in my head, but I print them all anyway. Desperation, fed by a nagging sense of obligation, keeps propelling me forward. If I can recognize one single face, I will have something: proof for myself, if not for anyone else. No faces meet this need and I've run out of gallery pages on the website. I scoop the additional papers into my stack and stuff it all in my bag.

A sense of failure swells in my chest as Patty and I return to her car. I have grainy black-and-white photos of unfamiliar people and a city that in no way resembles Vancouver. The images look like any generic Wild West town with no recognizable landmarks. I feel nothing new or unusual looking at the pictures. Once I'm not so bummed out, I'll look again more carefully.

Chapter 10

*F*inding my diary back on my nightstand as my alarm wails intermittent cries of EEEE ... EEEE ... EEEE ... at seven a.m. sends a chill down my spine. I no longer suspect Rayanne, but it is risky to have it out regardless. My pulse races as I check the back of the book to see if my library photos are still tucked in the back where I left them. They are there: one, two, three, four, all of them. I stuff the whole book under the waistband of my sweatpants and head for the bathroom to read.

My first night on the street was very nearly unbearable. I have still not come to terms with Sanjay being stuck aboard the ship, but I have good news. I have met a man who runs a home for disadvantaged girls. I will be able to stay here until I learn more about what is happening to Sanjay and our ship. The other girls in this home appear to come from rough backgrounds. There are few smiles here. Life in Canada must be harder than I imagined, but it was naïve to expect that everyone here led an idyllic life with a mountainside homestead. I must not think too much about the future right now. So many

*things must happen before Sanjay and I can be together
again. I hope my new friend will help.*

The entry seems to predate Akasha's letter and the
incident with her oppressor on the clifftop. She might
have bounced around a bit after finding her way onto
the old Vancouver docks. I still have no way to know. Do
I really expect everything Akasha tells me to come
through in neat chronological order?

"Katelyn, hurry up! Some of us have to pee!" shouts
Yolanda as she raps on the bathroom door.

"Coming, sorry! Almost done." I stuff the book back
down the front of my sweatpants and flush the toilet to
complete the ruse. I exit and Yolanda pushes past me
without a word.

Rayanne is still sleeping when I return to our room.
She is not yet required to adhere to our daily schedule.
She must still be detoxing, but she hasn't told me and
I'm not allowed to ask. I'm jealous that she gets to sleep
in, but I don't envy anything else about her life. Since
meeting Rayanne, I have wondered what led her down
a road that included so many drugs. Why do it the first
time when we all know what it can lead to? How sad do
you have to be to want to risk it all to escape? Or was
she stupid enough to think it wouldn't affect her?

Everyone else is at the table for breakfast. We are as
pleasant, yet distant, as we've ever been. Perhaps we all
view Arbutus House as temporary, so we don't bother

with connections. We all help clear the table. It is my turn to wash dishes, which I don't mind. I can linger in the kitchen, staring out the window at the tree-lined street outside without anyone questioning the use of my time.

I finish drying my hands after setting the last of the cutlery to dry. My phone jingles in my pocket with the generic tone that signals a text from someone not on my contacts list. It must be Patty. I swipe my finger across the glass to open the device and punch in my password. I had never bothered with a password until Arbutus House. After the initial gratitude wore off at being allowed to keep my phone, I realized other girls might not have the same privilege and my phone would be a lifeline worth poaching.

I find a message from 604-555-2435: *On my way soon. Can you be ready for 9 AM?* If I move quickly, I can pull it together in time, so I hurry back to my room to change and brush my hair. Rayanne is in the bathroom. I seize the opportunity to stuff my diary in my bag on the off chance referencing the photos may be useful.

My phone jingles again; Patty is outside. I grab my bag and get Mariah to punch my pass card again. I assure her that I'll be home for my four o'clock appointment with Jane.

"Where to first?" says Patty as I hop in the car.

"I have no idea. That's what makes this all so frustrating. I've got pictures of pre–First World War Vancouver and no way to connect the images to the city as it is. It's like looking for a needle in a haystack that rotted away a hundred years ago."

"Why don't we go back to Gastown and work our way south? If we're looking for old buildings, that's probably our best bet for finding anything in the downtown area with heritage status." As Patty pulls out into traffic I can't help but smile at her enthusiasm for my cause. I need an ally.

"The first time I went to Gastown, I saw a tile mural on the ground in a park. It was a picture of the *Komagata Maru*. Mom thought I was grasping at the first thing I saw, but I knew it was connected to Akasha. I saw in my dreams and in my diary that she came over on a steamship that was stuck in the harbor. And there was that website about the whole incident, but I haven't found anything that proves — to me, or anyone else — that what I'm experiencing is real. Maybe I really am nuts." I look at the dusty floor mat on the passenger side of Patty's car.

"You're not nuts, so let's have no more of that talk. Do you want to go back to this park? I think I know the one you mean, between Gastown and the Port of Vancouver." Patty is taking a different route out of Kitsilano today. She heads straight to the coast where we can see the city.

"I don't think that'll help. What I'd really like to find is the house I think Akasha lived in for a while after she got off the streets. She wrote a letter home and stuffed it behind a brick in the mantel above the fireplace. If that house is still there and the letter is too, that could be my ticket." Even though Patty's bought in, I can't help feeling ridiculous at saying my thoughts out loud.

"You know the likelihood of that is extremely small. Let's say your dreams and diary entries are all one hundred percent accurate. That won't help bring back a house that was torn down in the twenties."

"Are there houses of any kind in Gastown?"

"Come to think of it, I'm pretty sure all the historic buildings there are more like apartments. If we want to see any old houses, we're better off starting in the West End."

Patty's route spits us onto the Granville Street Bridge again. Instead of heading to the downtown core, she veers left to an area with apartment buildings, shops, and standalone homes. A few houses look like they could be old enough to be Akasha's refuge, but they've been upgraded over the years, so it's hard to tell. Patty parks in front of a home with a sign on the lawn for Greene House Museum.

"I don't think this is it," I say as I look up at the house, not feeling the twinge in my gut I think should be present.

"Will you know it from the outside?"

"I guess not. I only saw the sitting room in my dream."

"I doubt any house still has a sitting room, but let's go for a tour anyway. This is one of the few old homes around here you can just walk into."

We walk up the steps and I feel a mix of frustration and elation. I am putting one foot in front of the other towards finding proof of Akasha. I am also sure this is not the house that will produce my precious evidence.

The exterior of the house is immaculate. Green wood siding wraps around two floors, separated by a maroon shingled awning over the porch. A tower-like structure juts off the side, topped with a maroon shingled roof. It's too fancy to be the house I need.

Inside the beautiful home, I'm instantly overwhelmed with the sculpted and polished beauty of the place. Claw-foot furniture, a piano, oil lamps, and old photos all transport me to Akasha's world. But this is definitely not her home for disadvantaged girls. I shake my head at Patty and we head back down the front steps.

"I feel like we're so close, but so far now." I clench my jaw and relax it again, trying as hard as I can to stay patient.

"Let's keep walking. We can't just walk into most of the other homes, but maybe you will know it when you see it."

"Thank you for doing this. I hope you know how much it means to me. I can't even talk about this with Mom or the girls at Arbutus House. Or Mariah or Jane, and probably not Bryce either. Mom got it in her head that I'm suffering from some condition and it just spiraled from there," I say as calmly as I can. We pass more homes and I survey them one by one.

"It's strange, really, how something so small can get

you wrapped up in the system. I've had clients in foster care only because they're from a single parent home and that parent has to go into hospital with no other family to take them in. I've seen kids arrested for stealing a car and held back in school because of time in detention. They go home to a social stigma they can't shake and it affects the rest of their lives. While other kids do the same dumb thing, don't get caught, and grow out of said bad behavior through the natural course of life."

"If I hadn't told Mom about any of this, she wouldn't have taken me to Dr. MacDonald. Maybe it is kind of the same. But I can't blame Mom, not anymore. I know she wants what's best for me."

I stop in front of a heritage home that has seen far better days. The yard is fenced on all sides by bright orange plastic mesh supported with rough wood stakes. Demolition will start soon from the looks of it. Hand-written fabric signs have been tied onto the fencing. "DON'T DEMOLISH HISTORY" and "Save Our Souls Through Heritage" plead with the outside world to intervene on the house's behalf.

"This is it," I say to Patty as I peer in through an orange-framed diamond.

"Oh, honey, there is no way we're getting in here. It might not be safe if we did."

"Couldn't we contact the developer? I could make up a story about doing a class project. That worked well enough at the library."

"If you'd ever had contact with a developer, you'd know the last thing they care about is a kid's class project."

I pull back away from the fence and read the signs of protest again. I rack my brain for another option. I may be willing to climb over this fence, but Patty is not. I will have to come back again another time. If the stars align for me, the people protesting this demolition will stall the developers long enough for me to break in.

"Yeah, you're probably right. And what if this isn't the house anyway?" I hope I sound confident.

"Why don't we grab some lunch? There's a great fish and chip shop with a view of the water above English Bay."

"Are you buying?" I smile playfully and for the most part, I mean it.

"For you, any day."

Over our lunch of battered oysters and cod, I concede defeat on finding Akasha's house, but I ask Patty to remain my ally. She agrees. This is the best of both worlds; I can pursue the house lead on my own, while Patty remains available for something new.

DURING ARBUTUS HOUSE'S after-dinner TV time, my phone chirps the tone I've assigned to Bryce. *Are you up for hanging out this Friday?* My heart freezes. So. Many. Elements. Am I free Friday? I do have a day pass left. Do I want to go out? With Bryce? Yes, of course. But his brother will have to be there. I slink off to the kitchen to answer.

Definitely, but I can't be out on my own. I need to be with someone fifteen or older and I can only go for a few hours. What did you have in mind? Would Mitchell be able to take us? I write carefully; I have to break the bad news about needing supervision, and I don't want to sound too excited. I need to come across casual, yet interested.

I thought we'd just grab a smoothie. Could show you around the Drive if you're into that. Come see my hood. I'm sure Mitchell can come too. Bryce wants me to see his neighborhood! Back in the hospital he was talking generally about seeing Vancouver. But home is where the heart is, right?

I wait a few minutes so as not to seem too eager. *Sounds like fun. Pick me up at 7.*

He writes back immediately. *Will do. See you then.*

And now I have a date with Bryce.

Chapter 11

The week between my lunch with Patty and my evening with Bryce is painfully long. I can sense that my level-headed conversations with Jane have served their purpose in convincing her I don't need medication. I have no idea what medication would do to my clarity of thought and I can't afford to find out.

Patty has come for a few more visits. Bryce has texted, checking in on me. It's nice to be in touch with them again. But it won't be long before I'm released from Arbutus House. Mom will scoop me up in a heartbeat and we'll be back in Nelson, on our own again.

Once I'm home, I'll have left behind more than just my leads on Akasha. I'll be right back to missing Bryce, although I still think I need a new best friend anyway — a girl for once. Mom will tell me it's all for the best too. Bryce will say we can keep in touch until I come back to Vancouver for school one day. It didn't work the first time and even if he does keep in touch now, it'll be because he pities me. The thought makes my heart sink.

My heart tumbles deeper into my gut when I think about Akasha. I'm so close now. Sure, her case has been cold for a hundred years, but there has to be something I can do for her. Why else would she connect with me?

At seven o'clock, I'm sitting on the front steps of Arbutus House. Therese reminded me how desperate it looks to be on the edge of my seat until my "date" comes. I remind her that Bryce is just my friend, but it doesn't change the look on her face. It would be perfectly normal to wait on the step for a friend, especially if I've been cooped up for too long beforehand.

At seven fifteen, Mitchell's car finally turns the corner onto Arbutus Street and rolls to a stop across the road from me. Bryce is in the front passenger seat, which is good. It would be way too weird to sit in the back seat with him while his brother drove us around like a chauffeur. It's much better if we're all just hanging out together. I waste no time in hopping up and jogging to the car. Mitchell smiles at me, although he doesn't have Bryce's visual charisma. Mitchell's hair is combed mostly flat, and his dark eyes don't have the same spark.

"You're late. They only let me out for so long, you know." I'm hoping to break the ice and soothe my own nerves with a little small talk. I get into the back seat and Mitchell pulls out onto the road.

"I had to battle post-rush-hour Friday night traffic to get here. So, you're welcome," says Mitchell with a mild sheepishness. Bryce turns to me and smiles.

"Thank you for coming to get me. They won't let me take transit by myself, so this is pretty much my only shot at getting out of the house without my mom, former nanny, or one of the Arbutus House staff."

"We wouldn't let you take transit anyway. Not in your condition," says Mitchell.

"She's not sick," says Bryce. His aggravated tone of voice cheers me; he's defending my honor, sort of. If only I could get over the frown on Mitchell's face in the rearview mirror. An awkward silence takes over until we turn left onto Commercial Drive.

"What part of the Drive would you like to see?" asks Mitchell.

"I don't know. I've never been on Commercial Drive on foot. Every time Mom and I come to Vancouver, it's all about downtown," I say as I look over the storefronts scrolling past us.

"Then you're in for a treat. This is hipster central. People are calling it just 'the Drive' these days. I think some marketer came up with that and put it on ribbons on every other lamppost and now the cool crowd thinks they invented it," says Bryce. We turn onto a side street and coast past cars parked bumper to bumper.

"It must be a cool neighborhood if there's nowhere to park," I say.

"More like Vancouver has too many people for the number of interesting places to hang out," says Mitchell. We turn another corner, now a block parallel to Commercial and finally park.

"I don't mind it being busy here. I'm a sucker for

trendy hangouts. Remember how much there is to do in Nelson? The tourists usually last a week and they've burned it all up." I'm using my best all-is-cool-and-normal voice. Deep down I wish Mitchell would stay in the car while Bryce and I explore the Drive.

"I remember. Vancouver may be crazy, but there's literally no end of things to do," says Bryce.

"Dad says the city will never justify the cost of real estate. I agree with him," says Mitchell. We get out of the car and Mitchell assesses his parking job, not satisfied, while Bryce plugs change into the parking meter.

"You guys don't use your phones for parking?"

"Listen to you. Big city already. Or has Nelson upgraded the parking meters since we moved?" says Bryce.

"Patty used her phone to pay for parking when we went to the library the other day. We went to the Central branch downtown."

"Good to hear you didn't just come to the city to crash in our basement," says Mitchell. His sarcastic tone and smirk suggest he's joking, but I can't shake the vibe that Bryce's brother would rather be elsewhere.

"Hey, why don't you go check out that model-building shop towards Venables Street?" Bryce says to Mitchell.

"Aren't I supposed to be chaperoning this little tour?"

"I seriously doubt the Arbutus House ladies will have any way of knowing if you don't stick with us the whole time," I say, doing my best to sound nonchalant. Mitchell eyes us both carefully.

"If you take off — either of you — I'm not going to cover for you."

"No worries. I've learned my lesson. I'm playing by the book from now on." I lift my hand in a pledge of truth.

"Give me a shred of credit. Just go," says Bryce. He's straddling a fine line between staying on Mitchell's good side and speaking his mind. The mind seems to be on my side.

"We'll meet back here in an hour. That gives you guys time to wander around and we'll still have Katelyn back before her pass expires. Don't get into trouble." Mitchell shakes his head and walks off.

Bryce and I cross the road heading in the opposite direction.

"He's really not excited about driving us around, is he?"

"It's not that. He finished the year second in his math class. Dad is not happy and he's making Mitchell study all summer."

"Ouch. Does your dad know why you both came out today?"

"Yes and no. He knows we're showing you around the Drive. He doesn't know you're in a home for youth. We left that part out. He maybe kind of thinks you're staying with your mom's friend." Bryce looks away. We need a new topic of conversation. We arrive at back at Commercial next to a pet store.

"So, what part of the Drive should I see first? This is your town now. Lead the way to whatever is awesome."

"Okay. There's a great gelato place around the corner."

"Perfect! I'm not much of a smoothie person anyway."

"So, how are things going, being at Arbutus House?"

I stop and think before I answer. If I tell the truth, I keep Bryce in the loop on the fact that I still believe in Akasha.

"It's tough. I never would have thought that having a couple of quirky ideas would land me in mental health treatment. Mom is so sure there's something physically wrong. I feel fine. I'm not sick or crazy."

"For what it's worth, I don't think you're crazy. Neither does Mom, but she won't say so in front of Dad." The image of Bryce's mother smiling in her kitchen flashes in my mind's eye. Radhika might sympathize with me, if I get a chance to talk to her and tell my side of the story properly.

We pass a spice shop, a clothing boutique, and a book shop. The window of an antique store catches my eye — its display includes a crystal ball resting in a ceramic dragon claw hand, a stack of tarot cards, a handful of runes, and a sun-bleached yellow-and-black Ouija board.

"Can we look inside?"

"Sure, we still have time."

The aromas of amber and sandalwood are thick in the smoky air of the shop. Incense has been burning here for a long time. A middle-aged woman with long flowing salt-and-pepper hair reads a book behind the counter.

"Excuse me, is the stuff in your window for sale?" I ask

her. Bryce browses, peering into the curio cabinets.

"What were you looking at?" The woman rises from her chair and walks to the window.

"I'm interested in the Ouija board."

"That's a lovely one, isn't it? Are you thinking of it for personal use or a gift? These vintage boards are pretty popular right now." I'm not sure if she's making conversation or trying to sell me the value of an item that's overpriced.

"It's just for me."

She hands me the board and an inverted heart-shaped instrument with a magnifying glass in the middle.

"This is called a planchette."

"How much for both of them?"

Out of the corner of my eye I can see Bryce frowning at me.

"Twenty-five for the set. You can't buy one without the other. It's bad juju to break a board and planchette pairing, particularly one that's been used for so long." The saleswoman has a deadpan expression I can't read, other than taking her at face value. I do not believe in juju, but my personal experience compels me to believe in the capacity of the dead to communicate.

"Would you take twenty? It's all I've got with me. My mom took my bank card. It's a long story."

The saleswoman hums and haws.

"I've got five bucks," says Bryce. He's still frowning, but he's already holding a blue bill out to us.

"Thanks. You don't have to do that," I say sheepishly.

My new used Ouija board is wrapped up and we're back out on the street, me holding a paper bag a few minutes later.

"Let me just ask this: are you going to get in trouble for having that thing? Not that I think you're going to accomplish anything, but you're supposed to put that dream and diary stuff behind you, right? At least as far as Arbutus House is concerned, yes?"

"They don't need to see this. They don't search my stuff and they won't unless I give them a reason. My sessions with Jane are going well. She'll be calling Dr. Werdiger soon to re-evaluate me for release. I know the difference between real and pretend, so I don't see the harm." My stomach wrenches. I badly want Bryce to be an ally, like Patty.

"I trust you. I wouldn't rat you out. I still think it's bizarre that you're in therapy for this stuff to begin with."

"It's because I ran away, remember? The deal with the almost-Amber-Alert and all that. Otherwise it would have been a simple visit to a psychiatrist."

"Well, at least you get to hang out with me for a while in Vancouver."

"Yeah, you're the real reason I ran from my mom and got myself on the hook for over a month of therapy."

Bryce laughs. I swallow hard and do my best to laugh with him.

Chapter 12

*I*t is a Tuesday afternoon in late July. I am in my bedroom at Arbutus House, unwrapping the brown paper layers taped around my Ouija board. I doubt very much that anyone's past life has ever made contact with this board. I feel silly as I lay the thing as flat as I can on my comforter. Perhaps feeling silly is what I need. If I feel outright ridiculous for long enough — and get no more messages from Akasha — maybe I can go home and put everything behind me.

Rayanne will be in a session with Jane for another half hour. I have time to commune, so I set the planchette down and place my fingertips on the edges. I've seen Ouija boards in movies; they're not complicated to use.

I concentrate and think of Akasha's face reflected at me in the mirror above the mantel in the Edwardian sitting room. Nothing happens. I open my eyes to a slit, looking down at the board. Nothing. I try again, eyes shut. I picture every setting where I have seen Akasha; we are on the boat, in the temple, in the sitting room again, on a grassy clifftop. I wait and concentrate, looping through images in my mind. Nothing.

"What the hell is this?" says Rayanne. Startled, I sit up straight and whip my head around to the door.

"I, uh, I thought you were meeting with Jane."

"Yeah, I was. Aren't you *not* supposed to be talking to the dead anymore?" Rayanne is far less understanding than Bryce.

"Are you going to tell Jane or Mariah?" My heart is racing, but my words are under control. There was always a chance of getting caught.

"Nah, you're good."

"It doesn't work, anyway. Not for me."

"Smoke a jay first. That'll put you in the right state of mind. You'll probably feel a spirit whether there's one or not." Rayanne laughs.

"I wouldn't know. I've never smoked pot before." Although Rayanne is a few years older than me, she still seems so young to be dabbling in drugs, even marijuana.

"Doesn't surprise me. You've got 'golden child' written all over you. But if you're into all this spirit stuff, don't let them tell you you're nuts. Just take it to the park so you won't get caught."

"I can't use a day pass without an escort."

"I'm fifteen. I've got a pass left. Let's go."

I open my mouth to answer, but I can't really think of an objection.

"Don't worry; I'm not going to smoke pot. I've only got a few cigarettes on me."

"Can I get a rain check? We've got the family barbeque tonight, remember?"

"That thing? My parents won't be showing up to eat hot dogs with my jailers."

"Well, my mom's coming, and so is my old nanny. They're bound to notice if I duck out."

"Fair enough. But I might not be around when you decide the time is right."

"It's a risk I'll have to take." I'm a little relieved, but a small part of me thinks she might be right. I'll need a peaceful safe place to make the Ouija work. On edge in my Arbutus House room just waiting to get caught isn't exactly the best way to relax.

THE ARBUTUS HOUSE family barbeque proves every bit as awkward as I expected it to be. The picnic table in the backyard has a plastic red-and-white tablecloth stapled around the edges like a fitted sheet. Hot dogs, freezer burgers, potato chips, and condiments cover the table.

All of us girls are directed to set the table and hang decorations around the yard. The back wall of the house gets a welcome banner courtesy of Yolanda and Melody. Therese and I set the table. As tacky as she comes across, I still have a hard time picturing Therese with her bright smile and porcelain skin standing on a street corner, offering herself to the night. Likewise, I cannot picture Melody irrational and talking nonsense. As I arrange sets of cutlery, I wonder if I am more like Yolanda, for running away from home, or Melody for seeing things nobody else saw. I try to puzzle out which of us will go home and put our lives back together and which of us will keep going down the roads less travelled.

Melody's parents arrive, followed by Therese's older sister. Yolanda's parents and brother follow. As she predicted, no family comes for Rayanne. I'm starting to feel anxious about my own guests being absent. On cue, the gate latch clinks again.

"Katelyn, how are you, honey?" says Patty as I look up with a mouth full of food. Patty leans down to give me a hug, but Mom hangs back at the gate to the yard, already chatting with someone while holding a supermarket vegetable platter.

"What's this? Did Mom make a friend already?"

"That's your friend Bryce's mother. We bumped into them out front and they got to chatting."

Bryce steps out from behind Radhika and Mom. I had completely forgotten mentioning the barbeque to him. The mothers turn and smile at me, both waving as though greeting a preschooler.

Therese glides over to Bryce and introduces herself. Bryce looks so confused I almost laugh. I'm curious about what she's saying, but Mom and Radhika close the gap to meet me.

"Hi, sweetie. Isn't it so nice that the Manns could join us?" Mom's obviously forced, high pitch enthusiasm gives away how uncomfortable she is.

"Is the whole family here?"

"Just Bryce and me," says Radhika.

Her melodic voice reminds me of the time Mom commented on the perfection of her English. Embarrassed, I reminded Mom that Radhika had been born in Canada, like her own father. Professor Mann had moved to Canada to marry Radhika, so he did have an accent. It could have been worse; Mom could have peppered Radhika with questions about arranged marriage.

"I see you've already got lots of veggie snacks. Why don't I just pop this into the kitchen?" Mom smiles and trots off to find a home for her vegetables. I'm left with my fists in my pockets smiling at Radhika and surveying the backyard while Patty chats with Mariah and Therese continues flirting with Bryce.

"How are you feeling now, dear?" says Radhika. The quiet concern in her voice makes it difficult to feel irritated.

"I'm fine. If you ask me, this thing is just a big misunderstanding. I'm not sick and I was just being goofy." I brush the whole thing aside to keep her from worrying and to prevent a drawn-out discussion of my mental health.

"Bryce told me the same thing. I'm just worried about you."

"Thanks. It's going well. I'll be going home soon." And then a thought strikes me. "Hey, this may sound odd, but have you ever heard of a steamship called the *Komagata Maru*? It was —"

"Yes, I've heard of it." Radhika cuts me off, a curious furrow in her brow.

"I thought you might have. I'm … looking into it for a class project." I can't imagine I sound convincing, but she couldn't possibly know why I'm really interested.

"I might be able to help. My grandfather came to Canada on that ship."

"Really? Are you sure? The research I've been doing says hardly any passengers were admitted."

"I'm quite sure about it."

"That's great. I mean, that you've got personal knowledge, not that your grandfather had to go through all that." I'm fumbling for an appropriately tactful response when Mom and Bryce simultaneously return.

"If you'd like to come by the house before you leave, I'll try to find a photograph of my grandfather, and maybe see if I have any letters or papers of his," says Radhika.

"Why would you dig up an old photo of Great Grandpa?" says Bryce.

"I was going to ask the same thing," says Mom, eyeing me with suspicion. Patty rejoins us and I feel more confident with backup.

"Just a class project. Totally harmless historical research. Patty also helped me the other day at the library." Mom's eyebrows lift. This is the first she's heard of it.

"It's no trouble, Becky, really," says Radhika, softly reassuring my distrustful mom. "A lot of boxes got stuffed in the basement after our move. I've been looking for an excuse to go through them."

"Speaking of boxes, remember I'm moving offices tomorrow and it's going to be a long day. Can we call it a night?" Patty stares Mom down while tapping an imaginary watch.

Mom and Patty hug me and say goodbye. Others are leaving as well, prompting Radhika and Bryce to do the same. I walk all my guests to the gate and quickly retreat to the back step. I'm in no hurry to get started on clean-up.

"Why don't you go see a psychic? Vancouver is full of them," says Melody as she sits down next to me.

"What?" I'm shocked that Melody has been following my personal drama.

"I overheard you talking to Rayanne in your room today. Don't worry, I won't tell anyone. If you can't get your Ouija board to work, you should think about seeing a professional."

Melody's use of the word *professional* leaves me struck dumb. I look at her for a long moment and nod slowly.

An hour later, I am lying in bed, my thoughts racing. What do I want to learn from a psychic? Should I ask about the house in the West End? Or should I say nothing and maybe get an entirely new lead? Am I truly prepared to have the session produce no results, further solidifying my return home?

To be honest, I do not fully and completely believe in Ouija boards and psychics, not any more than I believe in crosses and crucifixes. Only the sense that I have come too far to let it all go keeps me grasping at straws. Confusion and frustration finally exhaust me to the point where I let sleep take me.

. . .

I am sitting in an old kitchen, at a small wood table. A plate of buttered toast rests in front of me. I touch the plate and push my finger into the bread. It's cold. I walk to the edge of the kitchen to look down the hall. The sitting room! I am in the Edwardian home!

"I have just the girl for you, sir," says the menacing voice I remember from the clifftop.

"If you'll wait in our sitting room, I'll send her right down," says the man as he walks into the kitchen. I hear footsteps clacking away from us down the hall.

"Oh, Akasha, I hadn't realized you were still down here," says the man.

"Yes, Mr. Calhoun. Sorry, I haven't much of an appetite tonight," I say. He walks past me through the kitchen and goes upstairs.

Moments later, he reappears with Estelle, one of the other residents of his home for disadvantaged girls. Estelle looks unhappy. She glances at me. She looks as though she needs help.

"Cheer up and get that wounded-puppy look off your face, girl. Your client is waiting. If I hear so much as a bad word about you, you'll find yourself working the docks," Mr. Calhoun says in a hushed yet angry voice.

My breathing becomes rapid. My heart thuds up and down in my chest. I rise to go upstairs to my room.

"Akasha, stay down here, please. We need to have a talk," says Mr. Calhoun.

I freeze on the spot. My heart pounds harder. I retreat to the table and pick up the piece of cold toast. I look up as Mr. Calhoun and Estelle go down the hall.

"NO, YOU CAN'T make me!" I yell as I grip my pillow. I am in my bed at Arbutus House. The room is dark. Rayanne groans. Did I wake her up? I hold my breath. She rolls over and snores.

I, however, can't get back to sleep. I get out of bed and look out the back window. What happened between that confrontation in the kitchen and the clifftop threat? What happened to Akasha after that? If she keeps sharing pieces of her story, I may not need a psychic or a Ouija board to find out what happened. Bringing her justice, on the other hand, still seems impossible.

Chapter 13

"I think it's time to talk about sending you home," says Jane.

I am sitting in her office for a session. I am anxious and torn about leaving Vancouver. Arbutus House is starting to suffocate me, but I am not finished. I can't let Akasha down and I'm certain I can't do anything for her from Nelson. Proving she was real and finding justice for her murder will take some form of hands-on evidence.

"I don't really think I'm sick, mentally or physically. I've never believed that. I don't have much control over my little episodes, but I would never run away from my mom again, I can promise that. I just don't know if I'm ready to go home," I say.

"I hear what you're saying, but given all the tests you've had, and all the therapy we've worked through, I think Arbutus House has exhausted what we have to offer you, Katelyn. That said, before we talk about ending your treatment, I do have some things to say I think you're not going to like." Jane is wearing a poker face. My skin prickles at the prospect of what she's about to say.

"I can't imagine what you're going to say that would bother me. I'm weird. I've heard it all before." I give a dismissive shake of my head.

"Before, we talked about your attempts to seek attention with your behavior. It seemed to me that your mother had to be the intended recipient. But after meeting with you both, separately and together, I don't think that's the case. Then I met your friend Bryce at the barbeque and I started to put the pieces together. I think you have strong feelings for him and you haven't been handling his move to Vancouver very well." Jane waits for my reaction. I can feel heat flooding my face. If Jane could tell, in one meeting no less, that I have a crush on my best friend, who else has figured it out? I've worked so hard to make sure nobody knows!

"How is that any of your business? What does Bryce have to do with my mental health?" I can't hide the anger in my voice.

"When did your condition worsen? When did you really start the strange writing in your diary and having these intense dreams?"

"I don't know, exactly. I've always had blackouts, you know that. It all got worse a few months ago, maybe a little farther back."

"I'm not saying you did this consciously or even targeted Bryce's family …" Jane is still talking, but her voice fades out of my hearing after the words "targeted Bryce's family" — as though I'm a stalker. I sit in my chair, folding and unfolding my hands, waiting for the noise to end and for her lips to stop moving.

"Do you think another two weeks here at Arbutus House would prepare you to head back home to Nelson?"

"I don't know. It's hard to say. Can we talk about it again next time?"

"By all means. You've done some good work today. I know I challenged you and it was hard to hear what I had to say. You're being very mature. So I have a home-work assignment for you. Do you still have your diary?"

Oh no! She wants to read my diary! I frantically go over in my mind everything my precious book contains. It's no use. There's no way I could share even a part of it. In a flash, I picture being forced to hand over the book to her.

"Yes, I do. I brought it with me when Mom and I left Nelson."

"Excellent. I want you to write a new entry in your diary. I want you to say goodbye to Akasha. Tell her whatever you want her to know, anything that feels like unfinished business." Jane's enthusiasm for this task compels me to ball my fists.

"Do I have to show you when I'm done?"

"Not unless you want to. A diary is a private thing and it's important for you to know you still have a private space. We would never cross that line unless we feared for your safety, or the safety of someone close to you."

I do find it comforting to know that she won't go

through my things unless she thinks I'm potentially violent.

"I'll go ahead and put the paperwork together for your release. We need one final meeting with Dr. Werdiger. He can refer you back to Dr. MacDonald in Nelson. We'll have your mom come by as soon as she's able. All we need is her signature and you can go home."

"Great. That's great. I'm looking forward to it."

MOVIE NIGHT TURNS out to be surprisingly fun. Mariah rented some cheesy eighties-era horror movies with special effects that were more funny than scary. In the Arbutus House living room, I finally feel like I'm in a room full of friends, not fellow mental health inmates.

Rayanne wiggles into the spot next to me on the loveseat. She has finished detoxing and is much more cheerful than when we first met. Well, cheerful isn't the right word; I am no longer afraid of her.

"Still got your Ouija board?" she whispers under the chatter of movie-bashing around us.

"Yeah, I managed to keep it hidden. I don't know how I'm going to get it out the door, but hopefully by then it won't matter. Jane's pretty keen to move me on out of here."

"I wish. But I've got an idea for you. We can sneak out tonight with the board and hit the park down the way. It'll be like our own spooky movie!" she says and giggles.

I'm pretty sure Rayanne just wants to smoke and she wants someone to keep her company.

"Uh, I don't know about that. What'll happen if we get caught?" I say.

"We're still minors. There's only so much they can do. Besides, it's just sneaking out. They'll never know."

Being caught sneaking out might be exactly what I need to extend my stay in Vancouver a bit longer.

"As long as I don't come back smelling like a cigarette. The last thing I need is to have Mariah telling my mom she thinks I've taken up smoking."

"Don't worry. We're gonna have so much fun!"

Melody looks over at us and frowns. I'm not sure if she can hear us or if she's just jealous that she's not in on someone's secret.

"When do you want to go?"

"As soon as Mariah's gone to bed, we'll just slip out the back door and around the side of the house."

"Have you ever snuck out before?"

"Here, or ever?"

"Ever. Like, when you lived at home."

"Of course. You haven't?" Rayanne looks at me with raised eyebrows and wide eyes.

"I've never had a reason. There's not much to do in Nelson in the middle of the night, especially for kids my age."

"Nothing you know of for kids your age."

I have to admit that if the popular crowd — or any

crowd, really — had anything going on at night, I wouldn't know about it. Other than Bryce, my friends are just acquaintances from school. I'm not going to share that with Rayanne, though.

"How will we know for sure when Mariah is asleep?"

"There's a bit of risk, yeah. That's what makes it fun!" Rayanne has a look on her face like she's talking about going to the mall or a carnival.

"Okay. I'm in. You lead the way when the time comes." Rayanne is right. I need to live a little.

Movie night ends and we retire for bed. Rayanne and I keep each other awake. She borrows my phone. She's decided to text a friend and ask if he'll come meet us. I'm suspicious, but if she's trying to score drugs, she wouldn't need to bring me along to do it.

Rayanne tiptoes to Mariah's room to listen for the heavy breathing sound of sleep while I wait in the living room with my Ouija board on my lap.

"If she's not asleep, she's faking it," says Rayanne in a hushed voice.

"Let's get this over with," I whisper.

"Don't sound so excited."

"I mean the sneaking-out part. Let's just go!"

Rayanne smiles as she carefully and silently turns the knob on the back door. The front door has a bell that goes off when opened and closed. But the low security at Arbutus House trusts the latch on the gate at the side of the house to keep us in at night.

We walk to the corner maintaining our silence. Any excitement at our escape could tip off Mariah or any busybody neighbors who watch Arbutus House for stunts like the one we're pulling.

"When is your friend meeting us?" I'm still whispering as we reach Cornwall Avenue and our destination, the waterfront park.

"You don't have to whisper anymore." She pulls a pack of cigarettes from her pocket and extracts one. Her lighter snaps on and she exhales a cloud of smoke. I follow her across the parking lot at the edge of the park. She is headed towards a pair of abstract stone knot sculptures.

"This is where we're meeting Kevin."

"When is he supposed to be here?" I ask.

"Any minute now. Give me your phone again." Rayanne's frustrated tone and deep frown make me anxious.

"So, is this guy your boyfriend?"

"Uh, you could say that. There he is!" Rayanne is pointing at a tall skinny boy with baggy pants and a large ball cap askew. He's just entering the park from a path ahead. A pool of bright blue-white from the streetlight above separates us in the dark summer night. Rayanne takes a step towards Kevin and stops short, her arm out to stop me.

"Don't move!" she whispers just as I see what spooked her.

"Sir, can you show me what's in your bag there?" says an RCMP officer. I didn't see him as we approached — his uniform is as dark as the night. He whips a flashlight up to Kevin's face. Kevin squints.

"Run!" says Rayanne as she bolts past me, back the way we came.

Fear nails my feet to the ground for a moment. The sound of Rayanne's feet draws the officer's attention and my fight-or-flight instinct kicks in. I'm pounding the ground to catch up to Rayanne. We're halfway back to Arbutus House before she finally slows to a walk.

"What the hell just happened there?" I yell.

"He … we … couldn't get caught." Rayanne is out of breath.

"Get caught doing what? That cop didn't know we're from Arbutus House." I realize immediately that Rayanne is talking about her and Kevin getting caught.

"What *was* in Kevin's bag? What did you almost drag me into?"

"Shut up. Just. Shut. Up." Rayanne's anger transfers to me as her words hit my chest.

We walk the rest of the way home in silence. Rayanne smokes another cigarette. As we near Arbutus House, I can see the living room light is on. My stomach drops through my core. I follow Rayanne as we retrace our route through the side gate and the back door. Rayanne closes the door quietly as we stand in the dark kitchen. The kitchen light comes on, briefly blinding me.

"Where have you two been?" says Mariah darkly.

"We just went for a walk so I could have a cigarette. We were only gone a few minutes," says Rayanne, dripping with exasperation.

Rayanne is telling the truth. I didn't use the Ouija board. This could turn out all right.

"I don't care what you were doing. You broke house rules. Day passes. Both of you, now," says Mariah. We both relinquish our passes on the spot.

"What's going to happen to us?" I ask meekly.

"For starters, you won't be getting these passes back any time soon. Katelyn, your release is probably going to be postponed. I hope you both had fun. This isn't summer camp! Get to bed now! Lights out immediately. Not a sound out of either of you," says Mariah.

Rayanne rolls her eyes, shrugs, and goes to our room. I stand my ground and open my mouth to respond. I can't think of anything to say. I'm suddenly very aware that I've got the Ouija board stuffed in my backpack. The damage is done, so I decide not to argue. I look at the ground instead and follow Rayanne.

As soon as we're back in our room, I slip the board and planchette out of my bag and stuff them between my mattress and box spring. I slip into a pair of sweatpants get into bed.

"Goodnight, Rayanne," I whisper to the dark. No reply comes. It takes me a long time to calm myself enough for sleep.

Chapter 14

At breakfast, Mariah confirms that my release has been cancelled. My session with Jane and Dr. Werdiger is still scheduled for this afternoon, so that should be interesting. Rayanne has fared much worse.

"Pack your things, Rayanne. An officer from the Burnaby Youth Justice Services Center will be here to pick you up at ten," says Mariah.

"No! You can't send me back into custody over smoking a cigarette!" says Rayanne angrily.

"I don't know where you two went, but you weren't anywhere on this property. I can't prove anything other than the fact that you broke the house rules. Adhering to the rules was part of the terms of your release. There's nothing I can do for you." Mariah's eyes are tired, her mouth a hard line.

Rayanne slams her cutlery down on the table and storms off. I can understand why she is angry. Nobody can prove where we went last night, or why we really snuck out. I finish my cereal in silence, despite my burning curiosity about further consequences for me.

I walk into Jane's office for my two o'clock appointment expecting a lecture. Dr. Werdiger and Jane are both wearing poker faces as I sit down.

"So, what's the verdict? How much trouble am I in?"

"We know Rayanne was the instigator of last night's incident," says Jane.

"We think a different approach is warranted in your case, Katelyn," says Dr. Werdiger.

"You're obviously not ready to leave treatment. What we'd like to do instead is have you participate in the Province's Kickstart program. The businesses involved specialize in helping youth at risk develop soft skills and improve employability prospects," says Jane.

"What's that?" I say, my forehead furrowed.

"With your mother's permission, we're going to set you up with a volunteer position at a second-hand clothing store downtown," says Dr. Werdiger.

"You have a couple of other choices through Kickstart. We could put you in a coffee shop on Kingsway or a restaurant in North Vancouver. Since you're not used to traveling around Vancouver, I'd like to place you at the location closest to Arbutus House, which is Visions Vintage," says Jane.

"So, let me get this straight, you're *giving* me a job? Just giving me one," I say. I suppress my excitement. I've often dreaded the day when I'll have to look for a job in Nelson. Unless I took a sudden interest in Girl Scouts or team sports, I'd have nothing on my resume once I was finally old enough to work.

"We need to consult your mother, but if you agree, we can start you as early as next week," says Jane.

"I think it's a great idea. I've never had a job before. Can I put it on my resume and get a reference?" I say.

"Yes, you can put it on your resume. But you need to be clear about the fact that this is not a job. You're a volunteer and you won't be paid. You'll have to ask the manager for a reference. I would leave that until the end of your time there," says Jane.

"Jane tells me she gave you homework to write to your past life in your diary, to say goodbye and achieve some closure for the delusion. Have you done this yet?" says Dr. Werdiger.

"I was going to do that last night, but then Rayanne wanted to sneak out," I say. I immediately regret using the term *sneak out*.

"Do it tonight. You can discuss the outcome with Jane in your next session," says Dr. Werdiger.

"I'm prepared to return your day pass if you're able to commit to using the pass properly and conforming to house rules from here on in," says Jane.

"I will! Absolutely!" I say with genuine enthusiasm.

"You've been making great progress, Katelyn. If we have no other slips, we can re-evaluate your release in a few weeks," says Dr. Werdiger.

"Thank you. You won't be disappointed," I say.

I leave my session with optimistic energy. Things have worked out in my favor; I have more time in Vancouver.

I don't want to wait until the evening to write in my diary.

July 28, Arbutus House

Akasha, I'm supposed to say goodbye to you today. You should know by now that I'm still on your side. No matter what anyone says; even if Jane goes back on her word and reads this, I'll keep searching. I'll find out what happened to you. I'll find a way to help you, I promise. I still don't understand why you reached out to me — or even if you are me — but I promise to stay on your side and fight for you. You deserve as much.

Yours Always,
Katelyn Medena

I close my diary, ready to return it to my nightstand drawer. Instinct tells me to open it again and find a fresh page. I pick up my pen, close my eyes, and picture Akasha's face. The familiar feeling of thick fog flows over me, but I don't sleep. I can feel my hand moving across the page; I can hear the faint scratches of my ballpoint pen marking the paper. I wait patiently until the scratching stops.

Sanjay, once you are off the boat, I will share this letter with you. I'm not sure what day it is. I can't see you or your father from here, but I know you must still be onboard. People have gathered to watch another ship arrive, a British ship. I do not know whether this will be good or bad. The men chattering around me seem to be amused that no one is coming off the boat. I think they want to see a battle. It makes me sad. I will pray for you again tonight, but I must also pray for myself. I may not survive sleeping out on the street much longer.

I wish Akasha would share something useful! A date. A location. What was the name of the British ship? Something I can look for! After I finish reading, I hastily hide my diary under my mattress. I caress my day pass. Suddenly, Melody's words from the barbeque pop into my mind. Should my next outing be to find a psychic?

I pick up my phone and launch the Google app. A search for "Vancouver psychic" brings up a few business listings. One, Madame Carolina's, is on Commercial Drive, not far from Bryce's house. I start tapping, *Can I trouble you for one more outing on the Drive?*

My phone stays silent for a few minutes, so I put it back on my nightstand. I'm almost asleep when it chimes for an incoming text.

Sure, how can we help?

Do you think we could ditch Mitchell again?

Probably. He was fine with it last time.

That's good. Because I want to go see a psychic.

My phone is silent again for another excruciating few minutes.

I forgot how much you like to live dangerously. What's the address :-)

Bryce rarely uses emoticons; he thinks they're tacky. He must really want me to know he's okay with humoring me. I'll take it.

I'm sending you the map link now.

SATURDAY ARRIVES WITH bright sunshine; Mariah and my fellow housemates are all cheerful. After breakfast Bryce texts me that he and Mitchell are on their way over. I am sliding into the back seat of Mitchell's car before the noon sun is overhead.

"It's going to be a hot one today. Make sure you drink some water while you're walking," says Mitchell. He's already in the loop on giving me and Bryce time to ourselves.

"I'm sorry to trouble you with coming all the way over to Kits. Thank you very much for doing this again." I hope my sincerity is evident, because I really am grateful to both Mitchell and Bryce.

"Don't worry about it. We're happy to help," says Mitchell.

"Mitchell doesn't think you need babysitting either, so we're good to go on our own," says Bryce.

We turn off Broadway onto Commercial Drive and reach the cross street just before the storefront. I didn't have the guts to make an appointment. I didn't want to be overheard on the phone and I'm just plain shy.

Today, I will be brave. Bryce is with me and I won't fool around with my one chance to do this.

The front door of Madame Carolina's is a glass window with a multicolored metallic tapestry behind it. A bell hanging overhead jingles as I walk through.

The space inside looks like a cross between a bookshop and a gift shop. Jewelry and crystals are displayed under a glass case. A sofa in the back corner is flanked by bookshelves. For a few moments, the shop remains empty apart from Bryce and me. A figure appears behind a beaded curtain next to the sofa and a woman with dreadlocks tied with a bandana pushes her way through.

"Good afternoon. I'm Madame Carolina. How can I help you?" she says softly. She seems friendly and welcoming, which makes me relax.

"I would like a reading," I say as boldly as I can manage while still feeling a bit silly. Bryce looks like he's biting his tongue.

"All right. I'm available. My table is in the back room. Your friend can wait out here, if he's so inclined." She eyes Bryce, a little suspiciously.

"Um, I need to ask: how much do you charge?"

"I charge fifty dollars per thirty minutes and seventy-five dollars per hour." Bryce lets out a sigh.

"I think just a half hour should do," I say. "Do you take debit?" If Mom knew what her recent transfer to my bank account was being used for, she would hit the ceiling.

"I accept debit, credit, and cash." Madame Carolina flashes a kind smile.

"Okay, let's do it."

Bryce flops down on the couch and picks up a magazine from the table in front of him while I follow Madame Carolina through the beaded curtain.

The back room is much cozier than the front. A single round table with two chairs occupies the center of the space. A sheer light purple scarf is draped over the single window, giving the room a violet hue while more tapestries hang on the walls. I look at a poster of a star chart on the wall opposite me as I sit down. Madame Carolina takes the seat across from me and places her arms palm up on the table between us.

"Take my hands. Say nothing unless I ask a question." I feel awkward as I reach out and place my hands in hers. She doesn't know what I want; maybe it's best if I don't give her any hints.

She looks me squarely in the eyes, and then she closes hers.

We sit in silence for what feels like a long time. She grips my hands and releases them. She groans softly.

"You are searching for a lost friend. She has run away from home, yes?"

"Yes," I say nervously.

"She came to Vancouver. She traveled a long way. So sad. So desperate. She is dead, yes?"

"Um, yes, for a long time."

"Shhh, no more. Only yes or no." I shift in my seat as I stare at the woman's lined face. She frowns with her eyes still closed.

"She is here with you. She follows you closely always. She has stories to tell you, but she cannot break through easily. The veil is thick."

"What's her name?" I ask bluntly. Rules be damned, I want a sign this is real.

"Shhhh, no." We sit in an uncomfortable silence. Madame Carolina grunts quietly. Bryce was right. I am getting ripped off again.

"Your friend has another name to give you. Eddie is the man." Prickles cover my entire body. My breath catches in my throat.

"Eddie. Can you find him? You must find him."

"Yes! I mean, I'll try. I don't know. I don't know how." My stomach lurches. Akasha must be giving me the name of her captor!

"We are done now, my dear," says Madame Carolina.

"But I need more."

"I work in half-hour blocks. Do you want to stay for the hour at seventy-five?"

I'm torn. I shouldn't be spending the fifty, let alone seventy-five. My bank account had ninety some-odd dollars last time I checked. If I'm wrong and seventy-five doesn't go through, I'll have to ask Bryce to pay her the balance. After taking his money for the (ultimately useless) Ouija board, I cannot do that again. What if we sat here for another half hour and nothing new comes through? It's time to cut my losses.

"No, we should stop here. Thanks, though."

Madame Carolina rises and gestures for me to follow her. We go back out front through the beads to find Bryce browsing book spines along the wall near the register. He looks restless and ready to leave. I pull my wallet out of my backpack.

"Please feel free to come back and visit me again," says Madame Carolina as I am punching buttons on her debit machine.

Chapter 15

The drive back to Arbutus House is a blur after Madame Carolina. My head spins the whole time with thoughts of Eddie Calhoun. I am certain the first name goes with the last. I spend the rest of the weekend racking my brain, thinking of resources and research methods that might verify his existence. Maybe a trail of bread crumbs will lead from there to justice for Akasha. I think about texting Patty to share my lead with her, but if Mom sees the message, she'll lose it. I will tell Patty in person as soon as I can. I hope she is still my best ally.

Monday morning arrives and I can barely concentrate on getting ready for my first shift at Visions Vintage. Jane is sending me on a city bus; this is a special exception as normally I'd have to be fifteen to go on transit without supervision. Neither Jane nor Mariah can come with me, so she's willing to settle for hand-delivering me to the bus and telling the driver where to drop me off. I'm not allowed to get off before or after Davie and Burrard.

The shop is not exactly downtown, as I pictured. I am back in the West End, temptingly close to the heritage home that teased me with possibility before. I force myself to concentrate on the task at hand as I reach for the door handle.

A digital bell chimes overhead as I walk in. The shop is not what I expected, surrounded by glass towers and expensive cars. Worn-out clothes, old books, grand-motherly jewelry, weathered paintings; Visions Vintage is a time capsule in the heart of BC's contemporary urban culture.

"Hello? Is anyone here?"

"Coming!" yells an irritated female voice. I am instantly on edge.

A short stocky woman with olive skin and a thick black braid flowing down her back bustles through a curtain next to the cash register. She is carrying a plump dark green garbage bag that she can't quite get her arms around.

"You the new girl?" she says, out of breath. She has a strong French accent. She doesn't wait for my reply. "You're late. Bad start."

"I'm sorry. I thought I was supposed to be here for ten a.m."

"Nine. We open at ten."

My pulse quickens as I realize I have forgotten the shopkeeper's name. Mariah and Jane both told me, along with the address and start time. The only information I have with me is a sticky note of the street number and time. Should I show her the note in Jane's writing? How could I be so stupid as to not write her name down? I have to tell her. I can't go on all day not using her name. I search her colorful tunic for a nametag. There is nothing.

"I'm so sorry …," I pause, thinking hard. "I will be here at nine for any other morning shifts, I promise. It was just a misunderstanding."

My new boss has recovered her composure and clears a space on one of her display tables. She upends the garbage bag and clothing tumbles out.

"What's your name again?" says my new boss.

"Katelyn. Katelyn Medena." My pulse is still racing and my stomach hurts.

"All right, Katelyn, I'm Noémi. I'm the owner, manager, one-woman-band, so to speak." A rush of relief cascades from my forehead to my feet. Noémi.

"Where should I start? Would you like me to sort these clothes?"

Noémi sizes me up, considering me carefully. "Yes. You give me three piles. One for throwaway, one for keep-but-cheap, and one for high-end or brand-name."

"I can absolutely do that."

"Good. I am in back until post carrier comes."

"What about customers? Should I help customers?"

"Yes, help customers! Any sales, you call me for the cash register," says Noémi. She abruptly turns and marches back through the curtain into the back room.

I am grateful to be alone so I can recover my calm. I

look around the shop again and back to the pile of clothing. Motion outside the front window and the glass door catches my peripheral vision. A couple has paused to look at the window display. The woman points at something and moves on. I relax further. I turn my attention to the pile of clothing and begin the task.

Piles for throwaway and keep-cheap build up quickly, but I can find very few high-end or brand-name options. A GAP shirt and a pair of Levi's jeans are all I have as I get to the bottom. The digital doorbell sounds and I look up to see Patty walk in.

"There's my little shopgirl," says Patty with a beaming smile. She looks so proud, but I want her to leave immediately.

"Hi Patty! I'm glad to see you, but I don't think I should have visitors here. It's my first day and I got here late by accident." I steal a glance back to the curtain.

"I won't stay long; I'm on my lunch break. I just wanted to check on you. Jane called to tell me she had set you up at Visions and I was delighted. This shop has a great reputation in the social work community." Maybe my visitor wasn't such a bad idea after all.

"Really? That's great. I'm sure Noémi will be pleased to hear that. Do you know her?"

"Not personally, but I'd love to meet her. Can you introduce me?"

"Before we do that, I have a new lead I wanted to tell you about. I went to see a psychic. Bryce took me. I got a first name for the brothel owner I saw in my dream. His name is Eddie."

"Are you kidding? That's amazing! How did that name come up?" I can tell from the tone of her voice that Patty is not convinced.

"She said my friend had a name for me, and the name was Eddie. It makes sense, it was the missing piece of the puzzle."

"Did she specifically mention Akasha?"

"Well, no, but she said my friend was there with us and needed to give me a name. It just has to fit."

"You were there. If you believe, then I believe you." It's tough to tell if Patty's encouraging me or humoring me.

"That means so much to me. You have no idea. Would you come back to the library with me? I want to go back to Special Collections and see if they have his name anywhere. If I can't find Akasha, I might be able to find Eddie Calhoun."

"Absolutely, we'll go. Should I pick you up at the house after I get off work tonight?"

"I'm not sure how this works with my day passes. I should probably ask Mariah first. Can I text you tonight to make plans?"

"You bet," says Patty as Noémi re-enters the front of the shop.

"Good morning, Madame!" says Noémi with a warm smile. "Are you being served?"

"Actually, I came in to say hello to Katelyn. I'm a social worker with the Province and I'm a family friend." Patty extends her hand to Noémi. The cheer drains from Noémi's face as she realizes she's not talking to a customer.

"She was late this morning," says Noémi as she takes Patty's hand.

"I heard about the misunderstanding. Katelyn has a great work ethic. I'm sure you won't be disappointed."

"I'll keep her busy and we'll see." Noémi smiles for the first time and I feel hopeful.

The rest of my first shift passes slowly. Noémi is not actually able to keep me busy. There are no more clothes to sort. A few customers wander through the store — a university-aged girl, a businesswoman, a group of vacationing retirees — but each time I offer assistance the customers decline. Noémi spends most of her time on her computer at the desk behind her curtain. Or this is what I picture her doing, based on the one time I poked my head back there and she snapped at me to get back out front.

I have time to think. About what it would be like to work in a shop as a real full-time job. About what might have shaped Noémi's gruff personality. About how soon Patty and I might get back to the Special Collections desk at the Central branch of the Greater Vancouver Public Library. Two o'clock arrives and my shift is over.

I manage to hold on to the thought of my library trip with Patty until I get back to Arbutus House. Mariah agrees to let me use a day pass that weekend. I have morning shifts at Visions Vintage for the rest of the week and she doesn't want me using a pass on a work day until further notice.

SATURDAY MORNING TAKES a long time to arrive, but when it does, I spring into action. I wolf down my peanut butter toast and rush out to the sidewalk to sit and wait for Patty to arrive. Our cover story for my mom is that I'm shopping for her birthday present and want a guide for downtown. Mom's birthday is a few weeks away, so the timing is perfect.

I still marvel at my luck in having Patty on my side, so much so that she's willing to lie to Mom. Whether she believes me or not, she's helping me, contradicting Arbutus House, and Dr. Werdiger. Even Bryce isn't that supportive.

Patty's car turns the corner and I am already running across the street while she parks.

The trip downtown feels familiar now. Morning traffic is light. We reach the concrete spiral of the library and park alongside it.

The library opens at ten. We make our way to the core of the spiral and up the escalators, back to the desk where photos and records might vindicate me. What I'll do with proof, once I finally get it, I'm not sure. I need to stay focused on finding proof before I let myself daydream about what to do with it.

A short, middle-aged woman stands behind the Special Collections desk today. Patty has agreed to take the lead this time.

"Hello there!" says Patty.

"Good morning, ma'am," says the librarian.

"Are you able to assist my niece and me with research for a school project?"

"Yes, what are you looking for?"

"We have an ancestor — my great-great-grandfather — named Eddie Calhoun. He was the first of our family to come to Canada, around nineteen hundred. We're using him as the top of our family tree, you see. And we wanted to find some kind of official document about his arrival in Vancouver. Maybe a photograph, if we're really, really lucky." Patty is masterful with her story. I stand silently, content to let her do the talking for me.

"Let me see what I can find. Most of those records are hard copies, but we do have digital records I can search. Come back in about half an hour." The librarian notes something on paper in front of her.

"Thank you so much," says Patty. She scoops her purse off the counter and we retreat downstairs.

Patty buys me a bottle of strawberry-kiwi juice and we sit at a café in the spiral's outer ring. I watch people come and go out of the library while Patty tells me about her week at work. I know I should be interested, but I am too preoccupied with trying to picture the librarian finding a photo of Eddie Calhoun. I hope that if I visualize the thing, it will come to pass and we will go upstairs to find her proudly displaying a photo of Eddie and Akasha standing in front of the heritage home in the West End. Patty will gasp. I will laugh. It's still a far cry from proving that Eddie murdered Akasha, but that will be my next mission.

We return to the Special Collections desk and I am vibrating with anticipation. This is the moment of truth.

"Oh, hello there. Sorry, but I wasn't able to find anything for you. Maybe try one of those ancestry websites. I hear they're getting quite comprehensive," says the librarian.

"Look again, please, there has to be something here," I say urgently.

"Sorry, dear, I've looked through both hard-copy and digital collections. We have no record of an Eddie Calhoun. Most of our documentation centers on buildings, monuments, government, and public figures. For random people, it's hit or miss. This one's a miss, I'm afraid," says the librarian.

I want to argue, but I can see that it's pointless. Patty puts her hand on my shoulder. My nerves won't let me leave. I realize how badly I wanted this, how much I'd come to count on finding something here at this library. And then I let go and walk back to the escalator. I assume Patty is following me and when we reach her car, I see her reflection behind me in the passenger door window.

"Take me home, please." I am out of energy.

And then a flicker of Radhika's face crosses my mind. She thought she had some family records related to the *Komagata Maru*! It won't connect me to Akasha, but it's something. How can I get her to dig through those old boxes as soon as possible?

Chapter 16

I have difficulty falling asleep as my mind races — about Eddie Calhoun and about the possibility of Radhika's family photos and letters. Should I keep digging? Should I let go, knowing it's an impossible quest? Will Akasha haunt me forever if I abandon her now?

I grip and release my pillow, turn over, and turn over again. I have lost touch with why I came to Vancouver. I had no plan apart from giving in to a wild idea. I thought something beyond my understanding had generated Akasha's writing in my diary and planted her dreams in my head. Perhaps it's time to start seeing myself the way Mom does, the way the doctors and counselors do. I'm a delusional child looking for attention. Having Patty, and when he's in the mood to do it, Bryce, humor me in my ramblings hasn't really changed the truth.

My frustration flows into sadness, and from there, anger. How could I be so stupid as to think that a past life wanted me to find justice for her? Saying it in my head sounded ridiculous. Of course my friends and family think I'm nuts!

My phone jingles. With Rayanne gone the tone echoes

in my quiet room. I snatch it off my nightstand, turn off the ring tone, and stuff it under my mattress to hide the sound of the vibrating. Phones are supposed to be off after lights out.

It's Bryce. *Want to come visit tomorrow?*

What? Had he read my mind? *I would love to come over tomorrow. Can someone pick me up?*

He writes again. *My mom offered. She found some photos for you and some kind of registration document. It's pretty cool!*

Is this for real? My heartbeat thumps a ringing into my eardrums. I take a minute to compose myself. I'll need to be even more cool when I'm at Bryce's house. Especially if Professor Mann is home.

Sounds great! Text me when you're on your way and I'll be ready.

I HAVE THE restraint to wait inside the next day. Giving up on Akasha has taken the wind out of my sails. Looking at some real-world relics connected to my dreams is going to be surreal.

Radhika and Bryce are running late, but I don't want to press them. Instead, I wait in the living room, watching the sci-fi B-movie Melody put on. I'm starting to pay attention to the group stranded in space on a cargo ship when my phone finally jingles. *We're here. Sorry we're late. Mom wanted to wait for Dad to head into the office.* No surprise that Professor Mann works on Sundays.

I shout goodbye at Mariah and anyone else who cares as I hop off the couch and bolt for the door.

Bryce smiles at me from the passenger side of his mother's maroon sedan. Her car is almost the exact same color as her lips. Not sure what I think of that. But Bryce's warm, bright white smile is more distracting. I'm still getting used to his trendy whip of black bangs and taller stature, which is noticeable even when he's sitting.

I slip into the back seat, slightly winded from having run through the house and across the yard. Radhika turns and smiles at me before she pulls the car back out on the road. I can still see her eyes in the rearview. Her thick black lashes and metallic-brown eyelids are much more glamorous than anything my own mom would ever wear. Radhika has always been careful to look good, and she's always successful.

"Mrs. Mann, thank you so much for coming to pick me up. I'm sorry I can't come visit you on my own."

"Nonsense, my dear, I wouldn't have you taking public transit. Through the city, at that! No, I'm only too happy to help," says Radhika's quiet voice. She's trying to speak up over the car and the street noise as we turn onto Cornwall Avenue, but she's still hard to hear. She says something else I can't quite hear, so I stay silent.

"Mom wants to know if you want a smoothie. We can stop on the way home." Bryce turns to project into the back seat. He doesn't have a problem with volume though.

"I'm okay. But thank you, really." I want to get to Bryce's house as quickly as possible.

Radhika finally parks in the small driveway of an old house. It's the quaint kind of old, like the heritage homes in Nelson, although our old stomping grounds feel very far away.

As Radhika opens the front door, the warm brightness of their home is breathtaking. The ceilings are high and I feel instantly out of my league. The faint smell of cinnamon and cardamom wafts towards us. We remove our shoes, and head directly to the kitchen, a magazine-ready showcase of granite counters and stainless-steel appliances.

Once we're sitting on barstools at the kitchen island and Radhika has poured us some tea and set out two fruit plates, I decide it's time to move things along.

"So, Mrs. Mann, Bryce tells me you found some pictures or papers I can look at for my history project."

Radhika's face lights up. "I hadn't forgotten." She leaves the kitchen and I hear footfalls on the front stairwell.

"Don't worry; the whole point of bringing you over was so you could look at this stuff. Mom loves her old pictures. But I don't think she's got a lot to go on. My grandfather changed his name at some point after he married my grandmother," says Bryce.

Radhika reappears with two pieces of fragile old paper to show me. The first is a grainy photograph. The second looks like a postcard. She holds out the photograph first.

"This is my grandfather and his father not long after they came to Canada. My grandfather and his wife owned that shop in the picture. I think it was a wedding present to get them started here. Very generous back then," says Radhika as she looked thoughtfully at the men.

"I'd say that's generous for any time. I'd love it if someone bought me a shop." I accept the photo from Radhika and cradle it in my hand as I look more closely.

The two men are smiling. One is middle-aged, the other barely out of his teens. It's hard to make out detail in the faces. They're wearing turbans and long tunic shirts. The black-and-white image makes colors impossible, but they're light gray in the image. A shop sign is partially obscured by the pair; only the word GOODS shows through. I flip the photo over. The writing on the back is Hindi.

I return the precious photo, which Radhika accepts and exchanges for the postcard. It's not a postcard, though. It's a ticket. Under a graphic seal and a couple of serial numbers it reads:

CANADIAN PACIFIC RAILWAY CO.
To the Commander S.S.————————

Please provide the bearer with Steerage Accommodation with food from HONGKONG to VANCOUVER. Fare ($50 Gold) has been paid to us.

Under the text is a PAID stamp with a date I can't read. The ticket has been authorized by a name, which is also illegible. And then:

Agents, Canadian Pacific Railway.
Calcutta 23rd December 1907
B. Hasan

And at the bottom, a name! B. Hasan. Sanjay's last name! Could this be any relation? Akasha has never actually named Sanjay's father. If he changed his name, was this the new name or the old one?

"This is amazing! This is a real piece of history!" Normally when someone is showing me old family photos, I have to feign polite interest. Pins and needles are shooting up my spine and along my arms. I remember myself and hand the card back to Radhika.

"Did you get what you need for your project?" Radhika seems eager to return her keepsakes to a safe place.

"Would it be all right if I take a photo of each with my phone? Just to keep a copy without putting your originals in danger." Radhika smiles and places both items on the counter long enough for me to click twice with my camera.

"Do you mind if I borrow some paper to make some notes?" I think better of it. What if I really was just looking at Sanjay and his father, and touching one of their actual tickets? Will I have another episode right here if I start writing? "Actually, never mind. I'll just tap some notes into my phone and email myself." I smile nervously. Bryce looks understandably confused.

After another cup of tea, Radhika and Bryce take me back to Arbutus House.

MY TURN IN the shower has been bumped to after dinner because of my tardy return from the Drive. I don't like going to bed with wet hair and the house hairdryer is broken. I'll just have to deal. But after a truly brain-blending afternoon, I decide sleeping with wet hair isn't something worth complaining to Mariah about.

I draw the curtain and turn the shower to mostly hot. I peel off my tank top and denim shorts. I step inside the steamy enclosure and pick up the communal shampoo bottle, cursing myself for not picking up some of my own toiletries during one of my brief outings.

As I work the foamy soap through my hair, my arms start to feel chilly. I turn the water all the way to hot. Stupid small hot water tank. They're supposed to be housing half a dozen girls here. Can't they do better?

The water starts to scald my skin, but the air around me is still cold. I start to feel nauseous. I need to sit down. Now. I flick off the shower head and sit down in the shower, hugging my knees for warmth. It's no good.

I pull the shower curtain back to grab a towel. I look over at the bathroom mirror and scream. It's not me! It's HER!

Akasha's face stares back at me from behind the condensation on the wet glass. Several lines are written in characters I don't recognize.

I STAND CEMENTED to the ground, panting. I break free and grab a towel. I need a picture! My phone. I wrap the towel around me and bolt out the door. I run down the hall to my room and fish my phone out of my backpack.

"Katelyn, what's going on?" says Mariah from the living room. I can't make out the words, but the other girls are talking too.

I run back into the bathroom and swipe my phone on. I snap a picture, although most of the fog is gone. A few words remain. It's still worth capturing. I take another picture and another. And then the mirror is clean again and I am Katelyn once more.

Chapter 17

I t is a beautiful, sunny Monday morning. I'm on the bus to Visions Vintage. I should be gazing out the window, reveling in the discovery of a potential connection to Sanjay. And I am … but the photograph and the ticket put me no closer to finding justice for Akasha. That's my only real goal right now.

I am, however, writing to Bryce to get a translation for my mirror message. If he can't translate it, maybe his mom will be willing.

I venture a glance out the bus window where the same old apartment buildings glide past. I add a message to my photo before I hit Send. *Please check out this photo. I think it's Hindi, but I don't know for sure. The fog cleared a bit before I could get my phone. Is it readable? Please help. I need to know what it says!*

The bus turns onto Davie Street. No reply from Bryce. I sigh and watch people going about their summer day.

Noémi is rearranging a rack of clothing near the front of the store when I walk in. She appears to be sorting by color and the effect is eye-catching.

"You are in back today. Many bags from the donation

truck need sorting," says Noémi, not looking up from the hangers in front of her.

"How should I sort: color, size, quality?" I am practicing my cheerful tone of voice for my next chance to work with customers.

"We do color this week, see?" Noémi looks up to make eye contact with me and makes a sweeping gesture past the rainbow of clothing in front of her. The look on her face suggests I am an idiot.

"Color it is. I'll be in the back. Holler if you need me." I am already plodding to the back of the store. I drop my backpack on the ground and slip my phone into the back pocket of my jeans. I want to know the second Bryce has an update for me.

I quickly create piles of blue, white, brown, and black. It's not until I get to the bottom of three large garbage bags that I have piles of pink, purple, yellow, orange, and green. I arrange the disheveled lumps in piles. There is no point folding until I know which will go on hangers and which will be piled on tables.

My phone doesn't vibrate until after my break. Bryce can't translate the message, but he'll get his mom to look at it when she gets home.

That's so awesome. I hope she doesn't think I'm nuts, though. I'll call you after work. I slip my phone back in my pocket before Noémi catches me.

The day drags on and on until Noémi finally tells me I can go at twenty after one. The next bus I can catch won't pick me up for another ten minutes, so I call Bryce. It's better to talk to him before I get back to Arbutus House and I don't want to do this on the bus. His phone rings and rings until he finally picks up.

"Hey Kat! How's your day so far? How did work go?" says Bryce brightly. He's trying to be polite. If only he knew how much anxiety is coursing through my veins.

"Good. Great. Awesome. So, has Radhika looked at my photo?"

"Wow, you don't miss a beat when you've got your teeth in something. You've never been one for chitchat, though, have you?"

"Okay, give me break. Lecture me on social niceties later."

"She's still not back from yoga. She left dinner for Mitchell and me in the fridge, so I don't think she's going to be back until later tonight."

"Damn! Well, please text me when you've got an update. I won't get the chance to talk on the phone again. I don't want them overhearing me at Arbutus. And tomorrow I'm going to the Vancouver Aquarium with Mom and Patty."

"I'll text you as soon as she gives me the translation. And I'll send her exact words, don't worry."

"Thank you, this means a lot to me. Really."

"I know. That's why I'm doing this."

After we end the call, the bus stops in front of me.

THE VANCOUVER AQUARIUM is tucked inside Stanley Park. The building is completely unfamiliar and Patty tells us it was recently renovated. We walk past a giant Haida sculpture of a killer whale and we're expressed through the ticket line courtesy of Patty's membership and visitor passes. I'm impressed again by a wall of rippled glass with tiny etched steel fish mounted on it. I love the Aquarium's glossy new makeover, but I'm a little sad that it's not the way I remembered it.

"I kind of wanted to see the old exhibits, but it makes sense they've got to cater to locals and refresh the place," says Mom.

"Me too. I wanted to see the place like it was when I was a kid," I say.

"Don't worry, most of the building is still the original structure," says Patty.

We pass through the vaulted foyer and through to the outside exhibits. A crowd has gathered around the dolphin tank.

"And this is Jewel, our youngest bottlenose dolphin," says a young woman in a red bomber jacket. Jewel the dolphin completes a somersault and drops back down under the water.

We are just in time to catch the rest of the dolphin show. Jewel and her friends dance and flip while the woman in the bomber explains what the bottlenose dolphins' calls mean, how much food they eat, and what their habitat is like in the wild. Afterwards, Patty guides

Mom and me through the rest of the outdoor and indoor tanks. Otters and penguins charm us with their play while beluga whales and jellyfish enchant us with their alien strangeness.

Patty treats us to a lunch of sustainable seafood and we catch the dolphin show again, viewed from outside the thick glass walls on the building's lowest level. An aqua glow radiates from the water and I forget for a moment that what I'm staring into is a cage for one of the world's most intelligent creatures. The thought of living in a cage for the rest of my life makes me sad, but I pull myself together and move on.

We reach a tank of Nemo and Dory fish, or, as I quickly learn, clown fish and blue tang fish. I peer in at the adorable creatures recognizable from a childhood favorite movie. The fluorescent tank lights flicker and then go black. The darkened glass is like a mirror.

I look at my reflection, but the face isn't mine. I am Akasha. I look myself in the eye. I touch my lip and Akasha matches me on the glass. Her eyebrows pucker sadly. She reaches out for me and I realize I'm touching the glass, leaning in as if to hear a whisper. The tank light flickers on again. My chest thumps. I whirl around, looking at Patty, who is smiling at the fish. Mom joins us.

"Sweetie, you look like you've seen a ghost," says Mom. Patty frowns at her. "Sorry, poorly chosen words."

"No worries. I got spooked when the tank lights went out. I'm fine," I say, smiling. My mom is getting no new information from me.

"Perfectly normal," says Patty.

"We should probably get going, though," I say.

Mom and Patty smile and nod.

Chapter 18

Arbutus House is busy with another themed movie night after my aquarium outing. I know better than to hide in my room during a planned activity, so it's not until Sunday afternoon that I get the chance to write in my diary.

August 3

Akasha, I need your help. I know I'm supposed to be helping you, but you've got to give me more to go on. I'm trying to figure out what you wrote on my mirror, but I need Radhika's help to do that. She's Bryce's mom, but maybe you already know that. I'm trying. I'm doing better than that. I'm fighting for you! I want justice for you, but I'm still fumbling in the dark to understand what you've shown me. I'm not greedy. Think of me as stupid. I need my hand held on this.

Yours Always,
Katelyn

I close my diary and hide it back under my mattress to wait for Akasha's answer — in whatever form it comes — or Jane's betrayal and my diary's discovery. It's certainly not the most original hiding spot, but I haven't been able to think of a better one.

I've managed to center myself enough for the evening ahead of me. Bryce texted me this morning after Radhika finally translated my message. But he won't tell me what it is because she wants to tell me in person.

It's an odd feeling to be leaving Arbutus House before dinnertime. Yet there is Radhika's maroon sedan outside with Bryce in the passenger seat, exactly as before.

"So long, guys! Enjoy tuna casserole night!" I hope I sound sincere. What I'm really thinking is, *Yay! No tuna casserole for me!*

"Say hi to Richie Rich!" says Therese from her perch next to the kitchen. I simply wave back at her over my shoulder.

"Good afternoon, Mrs. Mann!" I carefully close the back passenger door.

"I keep asking you to call me Radhika. You're old enough now."

"Yeah, I've been calling your mom Becky for a couple of years," says Bryce.

"That's different," I reply.

"Why?" says Radhika. I can't tell the truth, which is that Professor Mann is not the sort of person who wants children calling his wife by her first name.

"Because I'm old-fashioned," I say confidently.

"You are not," says Bryce.

"Speaking of old-fashioned, what was the translation for the writing I found on my bathroom mirror?"

"Somebody in that house of yours speaks Hindi and thinks you stole something from her," says Radhika.

"What? Neither of those things is possible. What did it say?"

"The words in the photo you sent Bryce say, 'Find my locket,' or at least that's the best translation," says Radhika.

How could a locket help Akasha's cause? There must be something hidden inside. A note? Some evidence? Where would I even start? Antique shops, naturally, but without knowing what I'm looking for, it's a lost cause.

We file into the Mann family living room and I experience the full impact of their house's beauty. The surfaces are all perfectly clean, from the moldings trimming the walls to the slate slabs of their fireplace. The eggshell walls have huge abstract art portraits. The ceiling feels even higher in the living room, although I could only guess — fifteen feet, maybe twenty. I had come here the first time with blinders on, focused only on getting a look at Radhika's relics. Now, I'm just here to hang out with Bryce, and tonight that means spending time relaxing with his family. Radhika beelines for the kitchen and Bryce excuses himself, so I sit down on the buttery black leather couch opposite a huge wall-mounted television.

I start looking around for the remote, but there's nothing. Not like I should start watching TV anyway. A large panoramic photograph of Vancouver hangs above the fireplace to my right. A huge bay window to my left shows me both mountains and city in the distance. Beneath it all immaculate hardwood floors — real wood, not laminate — feels warm under my sock feet. I will not be asking Professor Mann what he paid for his house.

"Katelyn," a deep voice says briskly and I flinch. "Come, dinner is ready." When Professor Mann asks you to do something, you don't dawdle.

The Mann family dining table is set with every possible accessory. A centerpiece of glass orbs inside a glass ball looks as clean and new as the rest of the house. Radhika brings meat dishes, roasted vegetables, and plates of naan and roti to the table with Bryce's help. We each get a bowl of rice before we take turns ladling food onto our plates.

Mom's most elaborate meals are dished up in the kitchen, onto mismatched plates, the same as any pizza night. In her defense, though, why get fancy when it's just you and your daughter?

I speak as little as possible during dinner, which suits Professor Mann just fine. He spends the meal quizzing Mitchell and Bryce about their summer study routines and extracurricular activities. I make a mental note to join a club or start playing a sport when I get home to Nelson.

Bryce and I both finish our meals first and Radhika notices.

"Bryce, hon, why don't you take Katelyn for a walk around the neighborhood. I'm sure she'd love to see the residential side of the area rather than just the shops on Commercial Drive," says Radhika.

"That's a great idea!" says Bryce.

"Only if it's all right for us to leave early. Shouldn't we help you clear up?" I say, specifically to Radhika. I have a feeling most of the household chores fall to her.

"We'll help when we get back," says Bryce, already standing.

"Don't start cleaning without us!" I say, and I laugh nervously. Radhika smiles. Mitchell and Professor Mann look at me blankly.

I fall into step with Bryce as he heads for the front door.

Once we're on the sidewalk and out of earshot, Bryce gets a strangely serious look on his face.

"I'm glad we got some time to ourselves. It's weird now that I can't come see you at your house — not really, anyway. But there's something I've been wanting to tell you. I need to confess."

"Oookay, you've got my attention. What's been bothering you?"

"I'd made up my mind I was never going to say anything, like, ever, and now it seems like we've been thrown back together even though I moved."

"Sorry about that, I guess I'm hard to get rid of."

"Don't interrupt! This is lame enough!"

"Fine, I'm zipping my lips."

"What I was trying to say is that I haven't been totally honest."

I'm on the edge of my seat, but I won't risk interrupting again. Bryce hasn't lied to anyone in his entire life, least of all me.

"I kind of, sort of, recently in the last year or so, started having a bit of a crush on you. And it's not fair to tell you now. I know it's weird. But I started thinking that I had to tell you before I'll maybe never see you again."

I stop walking and look at him with disbelief.

"I would have asked you to be my girlfriend, even after I found out I was moving. My dad would lose his mind if he ever found out, but it's not just that. I'm not ready to have a real girlfriend, but I wanted you to know. It's always been you."

My heart and my lungs are sparring in my chest. I don't know what to say; I couldn't speak if I did know.

"Uh, I'm, uh, sorry if I freaked you out there." Bryce looks down, rubbing the back of his neck nervously.

"I'm just amazed you didn't know I feel the same way. I've had a crush on you since forever. I was so sure you didn't think of me like that, so I did everything I could to hide it." The confession alone is like an anvil being lifted from my shoulders.

He looks at me for a long moment, as though an inner debate is bouncing around in his head.

"Okay. Cool." Bryce smiles awkwardly and I return the gesture. "We should get back. Mitchell is driving you home and he likes to get to bed early."

We start walking back and I grab Bryce's hand. I interlace my fingers in his and he squeezes. I'll take it.

Chapter 19

I want to leave Arbutus House as soon as I wake up and spend the whole day with Bryce. If we were both back home in Nelson, that is exactly what we would do. I would pack my bag with my bathing suit, a towel, and some cash. Bryce would come over for one of my mom's pancake breakfasts in our sunny kitchen nook. Then, after I begged her the night before, Mom would drive us north to the hot springs and we would soak and sun ourselves while Mom read a book. We would crawl into the cozy cave off the main hot pool. Bryce would hold my hand and put his arm around me until the heat and humidity of the cave made us dizzy. But we're not home and we're not free to do as we please. My phone jingles and I smile. I'll settle for a flurry of texts.

What are you up to today? Your mom is busy with work and I've got the day off. Patty's cheerful message is a small let down. My heart sinks another notch realizing how selfish I'm being. Of course I want to spend time with Patty.

I don't have plans, but guess what! I've got a new lead on Akasha! It's a long story, but I think somewhere in Vancouver a locket from around 1914 is going to help me. I tap madly on my phone, hoping Patty will be excited too.

Sold! Let's go antiquing and look for lockets! I'll pick you up at 11. We can do lunch and then search. I smile at Patty's unconditional support.

Yay! Thank you! Antiquing sounds like fun.

I change from pajamas into regular clothes. I rush to the bathroom for a face wash and hairstyle before I bound into the kitchen for a bowl of cereal.

Patty arrives ten minutes early, which suits me perfectly as I am raring to go. She's done her research and tells me Vancouver's antiques are scattered about the city, many focused mostly on furniture.

"New Westminster has a great antique strip too, and I think we might see some jewelry there. It's a bit farther away, but we've got a whole day to kill," says Patty.

"Six hours for me. I'm still on day passes," I say.

"Right, well, I'm sure we can be there and back in six hours," says Patty.

We clip along Broadway Avenue until we reach Kingsway Road, another major artery, and Patty turns right. We continue starting and stopping in the long-weekend traffic until we finally turn down a hill and pass into New Westminster. The surroundings quickly remind me of Nelson; the heritage homes are less manicured than Kitsilano and the towers are more modest.

At the end of the hill I can see the river ahead. Patty turns into a parking lot overlooking railroad tracks and a shopping complex. I am optimistic that Patty picked a good spot to hunt.

We park and make our way down to a street built partially underground, shielded from the main road by a steep grade and the old buildings above.

"This used to be the loading dock for a prison down the road," says Patty.

"Really? When was that?"

"Late eighteen hundreds, I think."

"That's a good sign. Do you think there are some shops around here that are that old?"

"We won't know until we look."

"Lead the way." I grin as I feel a hint of mischief bubbling to the surface.

I follow Patty into a shop with retro furniture in the window. It does not appear to be a shop that carries jewelry, but we have quite a few more to go before the strip of stores runs out.

"I remember these chairs," says Patty as she sits in a vinyl dining chair. "We had a kitchen table and chairs set just like this when I was a little girl. Back in the seventies, long, long ago."

I browse a china cabinet full of old soda bottles and mason jars. A tall man with snow-white hair and beard looks at us over his spectacles. I am uncomfortable, but Patty doesn't seem to notice.

"I had a doll house just like this," says Patty as we make our way to the back of the store. I have given up looking for jewelry in this particular shop.

My phone jingles. It's Bryce! *What are you doing today?*

Damn it! I am stuck with Patty for several more hours. It would be rude to cut our antiquing short and ask her to drop me off at Bryce's. My heart wrenches. I will be back at Visions Vintage tomorrow and may not see him for the rest of the week. What an agonizing week it will be. I twist and turn on the spot as I tap out my response.

I'm already out with Patty. We're antiquing. I'll ask if I can have a visitor at Arbutus when I get home.

"Hey, no phone distractions. You're hanging out with me!" says Patty. Her voice has a tone of mock hurt and I am embarrassed.

"Sorry, sorry. Just texting Bryce," I say.

"Look at this bear. This is a Care Bear. Do you remember these?" says Patty as she holds a brown stuffed bear with a red heart on its chest.

"I think they made a comeback when I was a kid," I am trying to sound interested, but I had never been a fan of Care Bears.

My phone jingles again, but I leave it in my pocket. Bryce knows what I'm doing now, so he won't be offended if I don't respond right away. Patty frowns and puts down the Care Bear.

"Aw, they've got vintage salt and pepper shakers. My aunt used to collect these." Patty looks at the little ceramics as though they were newborn kittens.

"Should we move on to another shop? I don't think

they have jewelry here." Patty's frown returns.

"Just a few more minutes. Are you in a rush?"

"No, of course not." I smile at Patty until she seems soothed. I follow her back around the other side of the shop.

We exit the store and turn immediately into the next doorway. This time we are in a purely furniture shop. There are no glass cabinets with knickknacks of any sort, so I don't look closely.

Patty takes her time browsing until she reaches a mirror with a carved wood frame. The border has the shape of a spiral and gleams with the overhead lights reflected by the varnish. A saleswoman approaches Patty and they start to talk. I hang back on a velvety floral loveseat and sneak my phone back out.

Bryce's message is waiting for me. *If you can't come over today, that's cool. Let's try to get together one more time before you leave.*

The last words knock the air out of my lungs. I'm leaving soon no matter how much I try to forget. Nelson seems like a crater, an empty pit holding nothing and nobody of interest for me. *Don't worry, there's no way I'm leaving Vancouver without saying goodbye.*

"Hey, what's the deal? Who's so important you can't be with me, here and now?" says Patty.

"Nobody. Still just Bryce. Just making plans." I can't bring myself to tell Patty that Bryce and I are … well, nothing yet. But someday, maybe something.

"You guys are still pretty close, right?" Patty looks at me inquisitively. She'd like me to confide in her, but the prospect of talking about losing my best friend all over again makes my heart hurt. A lump in my throat blocks my voice. It doesn't matter because I can't think of anything to say.

"I know you've had a tough few months, kiddo. Let's go find you a locket." Patty smiles warmly and softly as though she can see the sadness welling inside me. I fight back tears and rise to follow Patty back onto the shady concrete street.

JANE'S OFFICE IS muggy with heat this afternoon as I sit in her sticky vinyl guest chair. I stare at the back of her computer monitor, considering an attempt to log on and see the internet on a full screen for the first time in over a month, when Jane comes in.

"Hello, Katelyn. It's been awhile since our last session. Tell me how things have been going at Visions Vintage."

"Fine, I guess. I don't think Noémi is very impressed with me, but I think I'm growing on her."

"Why don't you think she's impressed?"

"It's nothing really. I think it's just her personality. Things are going great there." I'm hoping to move on and wrap up our talk. My failed jewelry hunt is getting me down, but I can't talk to Jane about it.

"How has the rest of your social life been going? You've been using all your day passes."

"Great. I've been seeing a lot of my best friend and my old nanny. It's really great having them both back in my life."

"Tell me about your friends back in Nelson."

"What friends?"

"You don't feel you have any friends or any social network at home?"

"Not really."

"Let's talk about some ways you can work on that."

Jane launches into a speech about how I can join clubs and sports teams through my school or in the community. I tell her I've been thinking about it, but I haven't made a choice yet. I'm looking for an activity I'm passionate about, something I will truly embrace. She agrees. Things are moving along smoothly. I couldn't be less excited.

$\mathcal{T}$he heat-wave weather has already seeped into my bedroom with the early morning light. The muggy air is perfectly still around me. The searing red characters on my clock radio say 6:10. Nobody will be awake for almost an hour, but I know I won't get back to sleep. This is a good chance to channel Akasha. I need more to go on if I stand any chance of finding her locket. Hopefully she'll understand that.

I pull my diary from under my mattress and pull my blanket back to give me a workspace. I smooth my fitted sheet flat and lay my diary open. Cross-legged, I close my eyes, pen in hand, and feel for the paper. The pages are rough under my fingertips. With my eyes closed, my sense of touch is heightened.

I take a deep breath in, trying to feel as calm as possible. I exhale slowly, noticing my heartbeat and sensing my lungs contract. I breathe in and out until the scratching of my pen starts. I don't open my eyes until my hand is finished.

The bruise on my eye will last for a week at least, of that I am certain. The fleshy lump on top of my cheekbone is still sore to touch. I think that was Mr. Calhoun's ring, but it does not matter.

Only the future of my soul matters now that I know Sanjay is gone. There is little left for me in this life. Mr. Calhoun tells me the Komagata Maru finally departed back to Asia. Only a few people were let off and he is sure Sanjay was not one of them. Mr. Calhoun tells me that if I do not start entertaining the house's gentleman callers within the fortnight, I will be turned out on the streets.

I am not ready to accept that I will never get home again, or that I must sacrifice my virtue for mere survival. Sanjay may marry while I have to fight my way back home. But is it so farfetched to think that I can work here in Canada to earn my passage back to India? Mr. Calhoun tells me I will not be hired by anyone in Vancouver. He promises to pay me a modest wage if I work for him, and that he is being generous because no one else would ever make me such an offer.

I am ready to run and starve before I give in to Mr. Calhoun. I have asked to leave, but he insists I stay. He keeps the front door locked day and night. This is for our protection. Now that I have seen the full force of his protection, I am harboring no further hopes that he means to help anyone but himself.

The only variable that remains unaccounted for is the method of my escape. I think I will ask Mr. Calhoun to take me to see the seaside, under the guise of agreeing to work for him and wanting one last special outing beforehand. I will be able to run from there. I will still need help. I will still need to find work. But the next person I meet after Mr. Calhoun is bound to be a better option.

Akasha has confirmed what I already believe. She was on the verge of being forced to work as a prostitute. I still don't know exactly how her life ended, but the scenarios are becoming clearer. Did Mr. Calhoun murder her or was it a client? One of the other girls maybe? Even if I could know for sure, I can't punish whoever killed her. It will be all I can do to prove she existed, let alone do anything to help her. How will finding her locket help me get justice for her? What does she really want? I angrily grab my pen and write below Akasha's entry.

WHAT DO YOU WANT FROM ME? I DON'T KNOW WHAT TO DO FOR YOU! A knock on my door stands me up with a start.

"Jane needs to talk with you for a few minutes after breakfast," says Mariah.

"Okay." I snap my diary shut. After Mariah is gone, I slip the diary under the mattress next to my Ouija board.

It's my turn to knock, this time on Jane's door after Mariah's satisfying pancake breakfast.

"Come in," Jane chirps brightly.

"You wanted to see me?"

"Katelyn, yes, I do. I have some exciting news for you."

"Really, what?"

"I have arranged for a hypnotherapist to come see you this afternoon. If it goes well, we can continue this avenue of treatment."

"Hypnotherapy?"

"I'd like us to do some work on exploring your deep feelings about your father. I don't think we've had a productive discussion in that area. Hypnotherapy can put you in a relaxed state that will allow us to talk freely about how you're really feeling."

I open my mouth, but close it quickly. We haven't talked about my father because there's nothing to say. He's not in my life. Who knows where he is? Not me.

On the other hand, maybe hypnotherapy can help me remember something meaningful from much further into the past, and maybe even something from Akasha's life. But even if it only reveals something about my past, maybe I'll remember an incident with my father and Jane can calm down for a while.

"Great idea. Do you need me home early from Visions? It's Tuesday, so I'll be at work today."

"So it is. You're quite right. You're usually home around two o'clock," says Jane. I nod. "Excellent. I'll schedule the appointment for three."

I'M BACK HOME just after two o'clock. Mariah has saved me some of the vegetarian lasagna she made for lunch. The added heat from the oven still hangs in the air and the humidity spills into the adjacent dining area, making the hot weather even more unbearable, but I am hungry so I eat quickly.

When I hear the front door chime my limbs tense. The hypnotherapist must have arrived. I put my plate in the sink and wash my hands before going to Jane's office.

The door is open and a tall, good-looking man is sitting in Jane's guest chair. He has his hands folded in his lap and looks at me thoughtfully.

"You must be Katelyn," he says warmly. His large pale blue eyes unnerve me.

"This is Matthew. He's here to conduct the hypno-therapy session we talked about this morning," says Jane.

"Nice to meet you," I say, holding my arm out. Matthew shakes my hand.

"Jane tells me we're going to talk about some behavior issues you've been having."

"What about my memories? Can you make me remember stuff from my childhood?"

"Memories are a funny thing, Katelyn. Hypnotherapy is more effective in helping you relax and control your behavior," says Matthew.

"So, that's a 'no,' then?"

"We can't dig into your past and get to 'true' memories, if that's what you're thinking. In your case, it sounds like some previous trauma may still be affecting you. But we'll focus on the present and what we can change about your future."

I take a deep breath. *Great, this is going to be a total waste of time.*

"Why don't you lie down on the couch? We only have Matthew for an hour, so we should make the most of his time," Jane says to me.

I follow her instructions and lie down on the couch. I fold my arms over my chest and get comfortable.

"Okay, Katelyn, please close your eyes. I want you to stay completely still and listen to the sound of my voice," says Matthew. "While I'm talking, I may ask you questions. You don't have to answer if you don't want to. It's more important that you stay in a completely relaxed state."

I decide to start by not acknowledging him and Matthew keeps talking.

"Take a very deep breath and hold it for the count of one. Good. Let it all out. Notice how calm your body is. You are relaxing deeply now. Take another deep breath and hold it for the count of one. Good. Let it out again. Notice how deeply relaxed you've become. Your body is floating on a cloud."

It's an interesting sensation, listening to Matthew's voice. I do feel relaxed, but that's because I'm lying comfortably on a couch. I don't feel spellbound. I don't feel much of anything.

"Now that you're completely relaxed, I want you to think of an object. This is your favorite thing in the world. When I count to three, I want you to tell me what you're thinking of. One, searching your heart. Two, visualizing your treasure. Three." Matthew pauses for my response.

"I'm looking at a gold locket. It's oval, but long. Like an Easter egg shape, but thick. It doesn't open with a latch; you slide out a piece from the middle and that's where the photos go," I say. I can see the locket in my mind's eye, but I've never seen it before. A rush of excitement hits me. This must be Akasha's!

"I want you to put your treasure in the palm of your hand. Hold on to it gently while we talk. If you feel upset, grasp your locket for comfort." Matthew is silent for a long moment.

"Picture your home with your mother back in Nelson. Imagine the outside of the house. You are walking up to your house and going inside. Your mother is waiting for you in your living room, but she's staring at her laptop. Your mother is too busy to talk to you. How do you feel?"

"She's working; that's fine. I can make a snack and watch TV in my bedroom." I'm not so relaxed that I don't see where Matthew is going. No more games for me.

"Fast forward to after dinner. You made dinner for yourself and your mother is still on her laptop. You had macaroni and cheese. It didn't turn out very well, but you ate too much anyway. How do you feel?"

"Full. I don't really eat like that, though. Let's say I made some fresh tortellini with prosciutto and tomato sauce with organic red peppers and fresh basil. Mom buys good food."

My eyes are still closed. I can feel my mouth smiling. I'm thinking of how good the pasta and sauce would taste. I'm also getting a kick out of thwarting Matthew's attempt to get me to whine about being lonely and ignored.

"Let's try another exercise. Let's count backward from one hundred, going as far as we can before we lose track. Take a deep breath and count with me." Another long silence from Matthew.

"One hundred," he says.

"Ninety-nine," we say together as I join in.

"Ninety-eight, ninety-seven, ninety-six, ninety-five, ninety —"

Matthew's voice is suddenly gone and I am back in the temple in India. The memory flashes and I am watching from a high window as Sanjay leaves the property. His father is waiting for him on the road. I feel a wrench of sadness over my whole body. Another flash and I am in Edwardian Vancouver, standing on a dusty road with Calhoun next to me. We are staring at a grocer's shop window.

"Katelyn, wake up, now!" says Matthew. He is shaking my shoulder.

"I'm awake. I'm awake."

"You were muttering in another language," says Matthew. His wide eyes are brimming with confusion.

"I think that's all we have time for," says Jane. She stands and gestures for Matthew to do the same. I sit up on the couch and reorient myself as Jane escorts Matthew back to the house's front door.

Chapter 21

I am in my bedroom at Mr. Calhoun's home for girls.
I am wearing one of his beautiful satin dresses. Someone has laced me into a corset, so I sit straight up in the
chair in front of my vanity.

I look around the room. The decor is beautiful. A
painting of a picturesque meadow is mounted on the
wall behind me. The headboard of my bed is made of an
oiled wood; I think it's oak. Light salmon wallpaper is
decorated with interlocking curved droplets. Each drop-
let is dusted with gold flake. The walls are like curtains of
sparkling water in the glow of my oil lamp.

The mirror in front of me tilts on hinged sides. It is
pointed up as though I were standing while looking in it,
so I pull it forward to bring my reflection into view.

I am Akasha, crisp and clear and close. My black
eyes twinkle in the lamp light. My long black wavy hair
falls like a veil around my ears and shoulders. I pick up a
large silver-handled mohair brush and begin to work on
my hair.

My hair shines, smoother and smoother with every
stroke of the brush. I put the brush down and pull my

hair back, separating it into three sections with my hands.

I braid until my hair runs out and I tie the end with a soft pink ribbon from the vanity's counter. The servant's bell jingles overhead. Long before my time, Mr. Calhoun had the house's servant bell system reversed and from the closet next to his kitchen, he can summon one or all of the girls in the house. I stand, smooth out the folds of my skirt, and walk away from the vanity.

Downstairs in the sitting room, my housemates are all lined up in a row, standing in front of the hearth. Mr. Calhoun stands in front of the piano on the far wall. My housemates are being evaluated by a rotund middle-aged man in a top hat. I join the line and meet his gaze.

I am the only Indian girl in the house and I stand out in a row of mostly white girls. One Chinese girl stands farther down the line, but the top hat is not interested in her. He smiles at me and I look down at the ground.

"I see you have someone new. She is a very exotic addition to your selection, Mr. Calhoun," says the top hat to my captor.

"Akasha is a very special girl, I assure you. A little lotus blossom," says Mr. Calhoun.

"I think I'd like to get to know her better," says the top hat, smiling more broadly. His decision is made.

Mr. Calhoun flicks his wrist, demanding that I come forward. My lungs freeze and I can't breathe. I look the man in the eye. A shaft of sunlight accentuates the orange-peel texture of his face. His bloodshot eyes match the ruddy hue of his skin. His white moustache twitches as he licks his lips.

I look at the other girls in the line-up. Their glassy eyes are lifeless. I don't even know their names. Mr. Calhoun has not permitted me to socialize, so I don't know how this life really is for them, but I can imagine.

Panic takes over. I bolt for the front door. It may still be unlocked from the top hat's entry. I reach for the doorknob and turn it frantically. The door doesn't move.

Footfalls close in behind me and I turn around. Mr. Calhoun has a ferocious look on his face as he reaches for my waist. He throws me up over his shoulder and carries me up the front stairs back to the bedrooms on the second floor. Mr. Calhoun throws me down on my bed and leaves the room. I hear the door lock. I sit up and recover my breath.

I stand up and walk around the room. My heart pounds and my blood races, tingling throughout my body. What will happen to me? How will I be punished? Will he strike me again? Will I be turned out on the street tonight?

A long time passes. I remove my gown and unlace my corset so I can lie down in comfort. Whatever the evening — or the rest of my life — has in store, I don't want to face it locked into a skin-tight cage.

I lay down on my bed and think of Sanjay. He will still be on board the *Komagata Maru*. Is he looking at my old spot behind the wall? Does he hurt as much as

I do? What is he thinking about? Does he believe me dead, drowned in the steamer trunk? Will he marry as soon as his father can reschedule?

I am too overwhelmed to plot another escape attempt. I let tears pour out of my eyes, not even bothering to rub them away.

A key in my door stirs me from near sleep. I look up and see Mr. Calhoun at the door. He locks the door again behind him. I am now wide awake.

"Akasha, it has become clear to me that you are under the impression you have options in your life. You believe that no matter what I have told you, a life outside this house may lay ahead of you, if only you choose to make it happen. I am here to tell you now that you are mistaken, my little lotus," says Mr. Calhoun.

He steps closer and closer until he stands directly in front of me. He caresses my face, but I pull away. He tries again. I flinch. He grips my jaw firmly in his large, meaty hand. He pulls my face forward to meet his. My fear satisfies him and he grins.

"NO! NOOOOO!" I cry out. I am sitting up in my bed at Arbutus House, panting, feeling around my body for the awkward confines of a loose corset. I am me again, but the memory of Akasha's tragedy is fresh and sore.

Moonlight floods my bedroom. I am alone in the muggy summer night. I get out of bed and take full stock of myself. I am wearing my old ᴛ-shirt and sweatpant shorts. I am unharmed, but rattled.

There's no way I'll get back to sleep, so I remove my diary from under my mattress. I walk through the kitchen and out to the backyard where the bare picnic table is waiting for me.

If Mariah finds me out here, I will tell the truth. I had a nightmare and need to write in my diary to get back to sleep. I open the book and start to document the dream as emotionlessly as I can. I concentrate so as not to let Akasha take over my writing. I want the information, but not the emotion of the incident.

As soon as I finish writing — it doesn't take long to stick to the facts — I go back inside and return to bed. I curl up, comfortable with my diary pinned securely beneath the mattress where I lay.

I cannot sleep. I stare out the window at the small patch of hedge I can see while in bed. I blink. I look around the room. I can still see Akasha's bedroom in my mind every time I shut my eyes. I keep looking at the moonlight hedge until daylight brightens the leaves and I get out of bed again.

Breakfast is a tasteless mush of milk-logged cornflakes. I say as little as possible to my housemates, pack my bag, and leave for work.

Visions Vintage is bustling with summer tourists. It is a mercy that I am too busy to think about my dream and the horror starts to fade, taken over by the immediacy of the real world.

On my break, I tap my phone and find a text from Bryce. I unlock and read, *Is tonight a good night for me to come see you?* I totally forgot to ask Mariah about having a visitor during the evening. Assuming he's allowed in, I'm going to be interesting company tonight.

Tonight's great.We eat at 6, so come by around 6:30 if that works. After work I'll have a couple of hours to corner Mariah and, if necessary, call off Bryce.

Unexpectedly, Mariah says yes to my having a visitor. She's even a little happy about it. I have just enough time to help clear the table after dinner when the Arbutus House doorbell rings.

Bryce is standing on the front step, smiling. I wave to Radhika before she pulls away.

"Mom's coming back for me at nine. I hope that's not too late," says Bryce.

"That's perfect.We don't have to get to bed until ten."

Bryce follows me into the living room. I frown as we find Melody and Therese watching a supermodel competition show.

"There's a picnic table in the backyard. Let's go there."

It's a warm summer night in Kitsilano. The mountains are a faint navy wall in the distance under the clear summer sky. Bryce reaches for my hand and I flinch like a hot poker grazed me.

"Did you, uh, change your mind?" says Bryce, frowning.

"No, it's just … I don't think it's allowed here." I look

at Yolanda, twisting back and forth in the tire swing. She's not looking at us, but I don't know how much she can hear. Or what she'd do with any gossip she learns.

I look into Bryce's warm, caramel eyes. He looks worried. Maybe I should tell him about my dream. It wasn't actually about me, so it won't sound so horrible.

"Also, I had a nightmare." I take a deep breath for courage.

"Yeah?"

"I dreamed I was Akasha again." I wait for Bryce to launch into an objection, but he stays silent.

"I was wearing a fancy dress — in the home for girls that took her in off the streets. I don't think I mentioned this before, but in the dreams and diary entries, it's pretty clear that Akasha was being pressured to become a prostitute. In my nightmare, the owner of the home for girls — it was actually a brothel — got really angry when she tried to run. He attacked her. It got bad. I woke up before the worst of it, I think." I am careful to tell my story as if I were watching Akasha, not being Akasha, when I talk with Bryce.

"Oh, my god. That's terrible. That's sick." Wide-eyed alarm flashes across Bryce's face and I hear the tension in his voice.

"It was just a dream," I say. "A nightmare. It's fading already. You know how some dreams you forget right away, but others stick around for a few hours, sometimes longer? That's all this is."

"Have you told your counselor or your doctor?"

"I'll probably tell Jane. Dr. Werdiger hasn't visited as often as he said he would. Jane said something about 'certified' cases taking higher priority than out-patient supervision." I look over at Yolanda who still appears oblivious to my conversation. I look at the windows along the back of Arbutus House. No faces are watching.

"Promise me you'll tell someone. You can always talk to me, but you've got professionals right here. Take advantage of that."

I wonder what Jane would make of a violent dream. A call to Dr. Werdiger? Medication perhaps? I'm not going to relate anything to anyone if the result will send me down a road of glossy little capsules morning, noon, and night.

"I'll tell her next time we meet." I take Bryce's hand anyway and force myself to hang on.

Chapter 22

"Hi, Patty," I say, answering my phone Saturday morning.

"I didn't want to put this in a text message, because I wanted to hear your tone of voice after my new idea," says Patty.

"Can this possibly be good?"

"I think it's good. I booked you into an art class. I ran it by Jane; she's not going to make you use day passes. It's Tuesdays and Thursdays for the rest of August, starting next week. What do you think?"

"Art class? Hmmm. Sure, sounds fun." Every extra moment I spend outside Arbutus House is worth pouncing on.

"Don't tell your mom or Jane I suggested this, but ..." Patty pauses to take a deep breath.

"What is it?"

"I thought you might be able to use the class to draw a portrait of Akasha. The art teacher is going to give you assignments, but you'll have free time too. I thought it might help you make sense of what you're going through. It could be cathartic."

"Wow, that's a great idea! I might not do a perfect job, but it couldn't hurt. Thanks!"

"I'm glad you're into it. I'll pick up the stuff on the supply list. Your mom wants to see you this weekend if you're not spending all your time with Bryce. Can you come over this afternoon?"

"Sure, I'll check with Mariah and text you back. I've been allowed to go to Visions Vintage by myself on the bus. Maybe they'll let me take the bus to come to you."

"If not, either your mom or I will come and get you."

ON THE BUS home from Patty's house that evening, her words are still swimming laps in my head. I never considered Patty a part of our family, but I suppose she was, or now is again. I'm going to take her up on her suggestion to draw a portrait of Akasha in art class. I might have more visions or see things more clearly if I could look at her face at will. Why hadn't I thought of that before? If it weren't for Patty, my life could easily have crumbled into a mess. It still might.

As I turn the knob of Arbutus House's front door. My phone jingles. It's Bryce!

Are you free tonight for a visit? Mitchell offered to bring me to see you. He's in a crazy good mood!

I can feel the broad grin on my face as I tap the glass on my phone.

I'd love that! We should get in as many visits as we can

before I go. Still don't know how long I have left in Van. Does 7 work for time?

Should do. I'm going to be so sad when you're gone. I'm glad I finally told you how I feel though! It felt great to know you feel the same way.

My heart wrenches, torn between happiness and self-pity.

We'll work something out. I won't get to come back to the Coast often and you'll probably never come back to Nelson, but it's the 21st Century. We can keep in touch :-)

I almost never use emoticons myself, but I can't resist.

You're right. We'll find a way to stay connected. See you at 7!

My housemates are all in the backyard enjoying the mild summer evening when a black Mercedes suv pulls up in front of the house. I squint at the tinted windows, trying to figure out what a vehicle like this is doing in front of Arbutus House. A moment later I get my explanation.

Professor Mann steps out of the driver's side and walks around the front of the vehicle. The passenger-side tinted window slides down and Bryce is sitting in the seat. He looks like he's been crying. I can't be certain from behind the living-room window, but a sinking knot behind my rib cage tells me I won't get to ask Bryce how he's doing.

Professor Mann marches along the walk and up the stairs to the Arbutus House front door. The bell chimes.

Panic floods me from head to toe. Why is he here? Why is Bryce so upset? Should I get Mariah? The bell chimes again. Nobody but me is inside the house. I get up and approach the door. Banging replaces the chime and I jump before I open the door.

"He-hello," I say, visibly shaking. Professor Mann's dark eyes glare at me.

"I am here to tell you in person that you will have no future contact with my son." Professor Mann's neatly trimmed moustache barely moves as he speaks. His accent draws me in while his words push me back. I stand and stare at his furious face. I can think of nothing to say.

"You will not text, email, call, or write to Bryce. You will never set foot on our property ever again or I will call the police and have you charged with trespassing." His words are filled with disgust.

My mouth is dry as I continue staring, frantically searching for some response as I feel my eyebrows lifting in disbelief.

"Acknowledge what I've said or I will enter this house and speak with the proprietor to ensure that I'm understood."

"Yes. I mean, yes, I understand."

"Good."

"But, why are —"

"I owe you no explanation, but at your age, if you have to ask, you're even more of an idiot than I took you for."

Professor Mann turns and marches back to his car.

Bryce looks at me. I'm shaking as I wave goodbye. Bryce doesn't wave back and Professor Mann doesn't turn around before he whips the car door open and tears off down the street.

"What was that?" says Mariah a few paces behind me. I jump again.

"My friend's father. He … I'm not allowed to see Bryce anymore."

"Why? What happened? Katelyn, you're shaking." Mariah puts her hand on my shoulder and I instinctively flinch away.

I meet Mariah's gaze and I see affectionate concern on her face. Sobs smack my face like a bucket of ice water and the tears flow. Embarrassed, I bolt for my room and shut the door.

I rip my diary out from under my mattress and violently shove pages aside until I reach a blank one. I grab my pen and close my eyes, feeling the tears still forcing their way through my eyelashes. I can't concentrate; I drop the pen and roughly wipe my face with both hands. It's no use; I flop on my side and let the waves of emotion crash down on my head. I hug my pillow until it stops.

My clock reads 8:05 when I'm calm enough to look up. I shove the cuffs of my hoodie into my eyes to dry them as much as possible. I sit up and breathe deeply. The tears are gone. My raw anger has retreated.

I resume the position sitting cross-legged in front of my diary, eyes closed, pen in hand. I draw air deeply through my nose and slowly exhale through my mouth. I touch the paper with my fingertips and think of Akasha's face. Nothing else matters. Nothing else is in my moment.

Scratching begins and continues for a few minutes, not as long as before. I look down to find a new message from my former self.

Mr. Eddie Calhoun approached me on the street again today. My presence on the streets of Vancouver has not gone unnoticed, or so he reminds me. His concern for my safety is not convincing, but he's right; I have few choices left. I watched the ship for another day. It has been another day of nothing happening. Chatter on the street is that everyone onboard the Komagata Maru *will be turned away. They, we, I, are not wanted. Why had it not occurred to me that coming to Canada might bear a risk of rejection? How could I have been so naïve as to believe that this journey promised my happiness with Sanjay and a bright future for us as a couple and, eventually, as a family? This country is a lie. I have to give up and go with Mr. Calhoun. I'll be trading my soul for food, but I'm too weak and too scared to do anything else. God forgive me.*

I knew Akasha had been forced by circumstance to go live in a house she knew was probably dangerous. Would I do it differently? The world of today is so different. If I became stranded, I would have options. The stupidity of running from my mom has become abundantly clear.

I close my diary and look out my window. Professor Mann's hateful glare flashes before my face. In a heartbeat, I see the dream image of Sanjay's father, Mr. Hasan, glaring down at me in the temple in India. This has happened before and will happen again. I shudder and stuff my diary back under my mattress before I climb under my blanket and shut my eyes.

Chapter 23

M onday was miserable, filled with moments of pure rage and wrenching sadness. I called in sick to Visions Vintage and wallowed in my room, knowing full well I wasn't allowed to shut myself in all day. I didn't care. And I knew better than to text Bryce for answers, but I tried anyway. My phone gave me this reply: *The Telus customer you are trying to reach is unavailable.*

Translation: Bryce's father blocked me and Bryce isn't allowed to change that. I spent most of Monday pushing away the image of Professor Mann's callous face, but it kept popping back into my mind. I tried to picture Bryce and all I saw was the image of him crying in the distance. Why? What was so wrong with two kids liking each other? How could it make that man so angry? And more to the point, how *dare* he speak to a child like that!

I haven't said anything more about it to Mariah. And I haven't said a word to Mom or Patty — I can only imagine what they would say. Mom might go as far as to call or even visit Professor Mann. That wouldn't go well for anyone. And also, I'm not ready to talk about it without crying.

I think I'll start by telling Jane in our next meeting. Hopefully by then I'll be able to talk without emotion taking over. If not, Jane will probably love seeing me cry.

Today is better, though: I have my first art class at the Kitsilano Community Center, conveniently located farther south along my regular bus route. The class Patty enrolled me in is called, "Uncovering the Artist Within." It's a class for adults, but Patty assured them I'm a longtime art student, like most other kids in Nelson.

The classroom is brightly lit, like the art room back at my high school. The white walls are a bit yellow with age. The tables are slightly battered from use, arranged in an open square shape. The countertops are chipped and stained. I smile, thinking about how art can leave its own footprints. A bowl of fruit sits on a small pedestal in the middle of the room.

I take a seat and look around at my classmates: two men and five women, all looking like they're in their late fifties or early sixties. They'll think of me as either a cute pet or an arrogant brat. Probably both, based on the varied expressions around the room.

Our instructor finally arrives. A man in his thirties with shaggy hair, dressed like a surfer. I am intrigued. It wasn't my money spent on this class, so if he doesn't know the first thing about art, it won't be a disaster.

"Good afternoon, everyone. Welcome to 'Uncovering the Artist Within.' I'm Reese Macpherson." The room is silent, so Mr. Macpherson happily continues.

"We're going to dive right in today with a self-guided assignment. I'd like to get a sense of where each of you are at before I finalize our lessons." I shoot my hand straight up.

"Yes, miss," he says.

"Katelyn. Are you saying we can draw whatever we want to start?"

"Yes, Katelyn, we're going to do a basic pencil sketch. Just a plain old number two pencil — nothing fancy yet. You're welcome to use the still-life fruit, but you can draw whatever you like today," says Mr. Macpherson.

"Thanks, Mr. Macpherson." I will be drawing Akasha immediately.

"Please call me Reese. My old man is Mr. Macpherson." Reese's surfer outfit makes much more sense now. I wonder if these retirees will appreciate his youthful approach.

Reese hands us each several large sheets of thin pulp-gray sketching paper. I unzip my brand-new pencil case and find a number two pencil.

Today's class is one of six sessions. I don't know if Patty and the instructor and Jane will all co-ordinate to review my participation in assignments (or attendance in class at a bare minimum) so whatever I can sketch of Akasha this afternoon has to count.

I look at the fruit, and then around at my classmates. Everyone has started to sketch the bowl and its contents. I'll stand out. Oh well.

I close my eyes and picture Akasha in her satin dress.

Nope! I try again to see her in her brown sari. The image isn't clear enough. I try again, this time picturing the temple and her colorful pink dress and orange pants.

I can't capture the color, but I start with her frame and build onto it. I do a quick rough sketch of her sitting in front of the lotus pond. I do another of her standing in the upper-floor window. It's not good enough, though. What I really need to capture is her face.

My third drawing takes much more time. I start with Akasha's hair and the gentle heart shape of her face. I work my way through the outlines of her eyes with their generous lashes and her full lips, shaded to capture their dark color. I fill out her eyebrows and tiny metal bell earrings she wore before she left India. The portrait isn't perfect, but if I want to take it with me without causing a scene, I should finish, fold it up and tuck it into my sketchbook. I do this and quickly fill in the next sheet.

I draw two faceless figures holding hands. They are Akasha and Sanjay in the temple. They were so happy for such a short time. Bryce's face pops into my mind and I fight to hold back the tears welling in my eyes.

"That's everything we have time for today. Please turn in your sketches. I'll get us started with chalk and charcoal next time."

I hand my sheets to Reese, nervous that he'll ask what happened to the portrait piece, but he says nothing, smiles at me, and accepts sheets from the round, grandmotherly lady to my right.

SESAME OIL AND ginger scents waft through the air as I walk in the front door of Arbutus House. Mariah has surprised us with homemade chicken chow mein for dinner.

"You're just in time to set the table, Katelyn," says Mariah. She doesn't ask how my class went and I don't want to open the subject.

"Dinner smells amazing. I can't wait to dig in." I mean it.

"I hope you like it." Mariah's tone is curt. Either she's angry that I haven't elaborated on the incident with Professor Mann or she's hasn't forgiven me for the incident with Rayanne. Or perhaps her tone has nothing to do with me and Mariah is a complicated woman. I know nothing about her personal life, assuming she has one outside policing wayward teenage girls.

Yolanda, Therese, and Melody wander in and we sit down to Mariah's culinary masterpiece.

"This is awesome. It's just like a restaurant," I say after my first few bites.

"You don't need to suck up anymore. They gave you a job and now you get art lessons," says Melody bitterly. I open my mouth, but no words come.

"You couldn't pay me to sit through an art class," says Therese.

"We know what they *can* pay you for," says Yolanda.

"Shut up," says Therese.

"She's not wrong," says Melody.

"GIRLS!" Mariah barks so loudly that I jump in my seat. She has gone from bothered to outraged.

"We will finish this meal in silence. The next girl who talks loses a day pass. Therese, it's your turn to wash dishes. The rest of you, go to your rooms after dinner. There will be no television tonight," says Mariah.

"What? That's not fair," says Therese.

"One day pass gone, who else wants to lose one?" says Mariah.

We all sit silently staring at our plates.

The meal has lost its zest for me, but I finish my plate and take it to the counter. I perk up inside as it occurs to me that our confinement tonight will work out for the best. I have a portrait to work on. Now that I know I won't be interrupted, I'll be able to work comfortably and truly concentrate.

I retreat to my room and get out my sketchbook. Akasha is waiting for me, hidden inside the folds of economy pulp paper.

Her face is beautiful; I'm not admiring my handiwork so much as feeling like I'm finally looking at her in the light of day. I captured more detail than I'd remembered. I don't know if I need to work on her any more tonight.

I touch the corner of her eye. I have captured her happy. I like thinking of her this way. A sudden sleepiness comes over me. My eyelids are heavy, so heavy. Can't … keep … them …

I AM STANDING on a dirt street in an old Western town. Someone grabs my arm and I look at his face. Mr. Calhoun!

"Take a good look now, little lotus. Your boy and his old man are here, sure enough," says Mr. Calhoun.

I focus on the shop window across the street where Mr. Calhoun is pointing. I can make out two figures moving inside. They are Indian men. The younger one walks out the front door with a sack of flour in his arms. The boy is Sanjay! He adds the sack of flour to a pyramid he is building in front of the shop window. I have never felt such a rush of happiness. The rush dies quickly.

"This is a miracle! Let me go to them. I would be a burden to you no longer." I have no confidence in my words. Desperation grips my heart.

"A burden? You are an investment, little lotus. And you will pay off if I have to sell your hair to the wig maker."

"Sir, please. If I could only speak with them."

"Know that you will never speak with either of them again. They would not speak to you, regardless. You are ruined to the people in their world. Here in Canada, they have no voice, no standing. Still, you are below them, below every other person on this street. There is no help for you and no future, there is only what I can provide." Mr Calhoun is both smug and deeply angry.

"I have nothing to offer you. I have nothing left to offer anyone. You've already taken everything from me. Throw me in the ocean and be done with it." I am completely serious; I want my life to end.

"I will decide what you have to offer. You have many years of value left in you. Your bud may have opened, but you will bloom for a long time to come." Mr. Calhoun grins maliciously and I feel nauseous.

"I will never consent. You might feel free to take what you want, but your clients will not be pleased."

"Stupid girl. Don't you know how many men will pay, not only for the exotic feel of your skin, but for your fiery resistance? Fight. Keep fighting, but learn your place."

I feel tears flowing down my cheeks. I cannot stop the sobs from rolling up through my stomach and outward. I clamp my hand over my mouth to muffle the sound.

I look around the street; we are out in public. If I cry out, will someone help me? I meet the eyes of a middle-aged man in a brown suit. He sees me crying, frowns, and looks away.

"Help me!" I sob at a woman in a pink dress with white flowers. She too frowns and hurries off.

"Enough of that, little lotus." Mr. Calhoun's grip on my arm tightens. I pull away, but his hand clamps on, harder, strong as steel.

Mr. Calhoun flags down a carriage and it stops between us and the shop where my beloved Sanjay is still stacking bags of flour.

I am forced inside the carriage and I seize my moment.

I lunge for the opposite door, pry it open and leap out.

No sooner am I back on the street than Mr. Calhoun's fist collides with my nose. The pain sears my entire face and I fall to the ground. Blood gushes onto my hands and I am hauled to my feet. Mr. Calhoun forces me back in the carriage and I collapse.

THE CARPET OF my bedroom floor is like steel wool on my face. I can still feel the impact of Mr. Calhoun's fist. I lift my head and force myself upward with the palms of my hands. I am groggy and disoriented. This is Arbutus House. *I'm Katelyn. I'm safe in Vancouver*, I tell myself.

The taste of blood still fills my mouth. I run my tongue over my teeth and flex my lips. There is nothing in my mouth but saliva. I rub my face with my hands and stand up.

The picture of Akasha is resting alone on my bedspread, which has a puckered impression where I was sitting.

I sit back on my bed and try to take stock. I pull out my diary and start to write.

Akasha, I am failing you. I'm failing us. What happened in your past — our past — is a darker tragedy than I ever imagined, but I'm no closer to helping you than I was the first day I arrived in Vancouver.

I don't know what to do! Is there anything I can do? Are you just trying to show me how horrible my last life was so

I'll appreciate this one more? That's where things are right now. I have no moves left. There's no way I'll find your letter or your locket. I can remember you and mourn you. That's it.

Chapter 24

Wednesday morning feels like I am made of molasses. Every movement is a struggle. I have to fight to find strength, to get out of bed instead of melting into a puddle. I call Noémi and tell her I am not coming in to work, again. I badly want to see Mom. It's time to go home to Nelson. I'm ready. If I can talk her into it, she can get me released, I'm sure of it.

Mom picks me up after breakfast. She could tell over the phone that I was upset, but I refused to tell her what's been bothering me. Not when curious ears are everywhere.

"All right, now tell me what's been going on," says Mom as she pulls away from the curb in front of Arbutus House.

"I didn't want to tell you on the phone because I think I'm going to start crying again."

"Okay, that's settles it. Whatever this is, you're telling me now." Mom ventures a quick glance at me, taking her eyes off West Fourth Avenue for a moment.

"I'm not allowed to see Bryce anymore." The shaking in my voice is back accompanied by an involuntary lip quiver. "Ever again. Professor Mann came to Arbutus to tell me in person. He hates me." Sobbing takes over and I can't get anything more out for a minute or two. Each time I take a breath to say something, sadness shuts my throat again.

"Take your time, sweetie. We don't even have to go to a coffee shop. We can just talk here." Mom has pulled off West Fourth onto a side street and parked.

Summer breeze drifts in the open window next to me. A pair of older teenage girls walks past. They look at my puffy red face and turn back to each other whispering. Yes, poor me. They're wondering what happened. So am I.

"I think Bryce's father must have found some text messages between me and Bryce. It was harmless. One night at his house, he told me he has a crush on me. I told him I felt the same way. Then we texted about it. That's all that happened. I don't know why that would make Professor Mann so angry, but he came over and told me that if I ever contacted Bryce I'd be in trouble or if I ever set foot on his property he'd call the cops. He was so angry. He looked at me like I'd done something horrible."

Mom sat there in silence for a moment.

"Does Radhika know about this?"

"I don't know. I tried texting Bryce the next day and I got a message that he was unavailable. It's the message they give you when someone has blocked your number. Professor Mann must have done it."

"I'm sure she knows. Bryce will be upset. Professor Mann probably yelled at him in front of the whole family."

"Please don't talk to him. Please just leave this alone. We should just go home now."

"I won't contact Bryce's parents if you don't want me to. But I think Professor Mann owes you an apology. If he doesn't want you and Bryce to be friends, he's entitled to his feelings. Given that you're going to return to Nelson soon one way or the other, I'm surprised he bothered to say anything, let alone to confront you like that."

"He probably enjoyed it! He hates me, I told you!"

"No grown man hates a child he barely knows."

"He's not your average man."

"If you really feel like Arbutus House has nothing left to offer you, I'll see how quickly we can speed up your release. Jane has already recommended sending you home."

"I know. Let's just do that. Really, Mom, that's the best choice right now."

"Well, do you still want a hot chocolate or a steamed milk? We could do a little shopping too. Won't it do you good to walk around and enjoy the city?" Mom's speaking in the high voice she always uses when she's trying to sell me on something I don't want.

I look up to the cosmetic mirror in the passenger side visor above my head. My eyes are red and puffy.

Red lines streak my cheeks. This will take hours to wear off.

"I look like a mess. I'll just be self-conscious everywhere we go."

"I could drive around a bit more. Why don't we meander around UBC? Who knows, you might want to go to school there one day."

"Driving, sure. School, don't even scare me with stuff like that right now."

The drive was relaxing, but I feel thoroughly gutted when I get back to my room at Arbutus House. It's the kind of exhaustion that only comes from a long crying session. I have a few hours until dinner, so I lie down on my bed on top of the covers and close my eyes. But sleep won't come. I open my eyes and reposition. My stupid brain is replaying both my afternoon with Mom and the horrible lecture from Professor Mann.

If sleep won't happen, maybe I can squeeze a little more out of Akasha. At this point, it's a desperate move, like looking on the same shelf over and over again as you pace back and forth trying to find lost keys.

My diary is still under my mattress. I pull it out and flip through the book full of pages that now crinkle with age and abuse until I find the last few crisp and flat empty pages. I've become efficient at tapping Akasha's memories. It takes only a few calming breaths before I hear my pen scratching once more.

Illness is certainly upon me now, but exactly what it is, I know not. I have been coughing for several days now, with my chest heavy and sore. I have woken at night many times, chilled to the bone or burning with fever and covered in sweat. I hope this is a passing trouble I can keep to myself and rest through. As I still refuse the work foisted upon the other girls in this house, I am left to do cooking, cleaning, laundry, and every other chore Mr. Calhoun can think of for me. I am biding my time looking for my opportunity to escape. I expect he thinks he'll wear me down by giving me too many chores. I have more resolve than he could ever under-stand. I will watch, listen, and wait. A viable option will present itself, and when it does, I will be ready to act.

Every time I learn something new about Akasha, I feel more empathy for her, but I'm still no closer to helping her in any way. I'm proud of her for standing her ground. I hope I never have to read a confession to giving in and selling her body. Either way, each new piece of her tragic puzzle makes me wonder how much is still miss-ing. I do know one thing; I can't leave this city without something to help her rest in peace.

Chapter 25

After my Thursday shift at Visions Vintage, I take a detour on my way back to Arbutus House. I have one last lead I can make a desperate attempt to explore.

I don't know the first thing about breaking into a house, but in the movies, they always "case the place," and that's what I'm doing to Mr. Calhoun's heritage home in the West End.

The transit website tells me there is no direct bus between Barclay Street and the corner of Davie and Bute where I work. But I don't mind the walk.

Akasha's news has been playing like a broken record in my mind all day. My customer service was probably lackluster at best. Noémi's approval of my performance places a distant second on my list of priorities today.

I think more about why and how Calhoun killed Akasha. At first, I thought it would have been him losing patience with her resistance to working for him — or he caught her trying to escape and lost his temper. Now it seems possible she became too much of a burden to him and he knew he could get rid of her with no consequences. Or maybe it was something different altogether.

If she became desperate, maybe she stole from him. If I can figure out what happened to her, I'll be one step closer to giving her peace. Am I selfish to hope some of that peace extends to me too?

I reach the Barclay demolition site and the house is almost exactly as Patty and I left it. The orange plastic mesh fence has been replaced with a sturdier metal fence made of heavy interlocking segments. New handwritten protest signs hang from it, but the message is the same, as I'm sure will be the outcome. The end is coming faster for this old house.

I peer in through a gap in the fencing. I wiggle my arm through with my phone to take a picture. It doesn't look extremely out of place for me to do this thanks to the protest signs.

If I weren't interested in breaking in, I would still stop to look at this house. The first time I found the house with Patty, I noticed the peeling paint on the wood siding and the overgrown lawn. This time, I'm looking at a boarded-up window on the side.

The fence will be harder to get through, but I'm betting there is no alarm guarding the house. Prying off plywood will be much quieter than breaking glass.

I walk around the side of the property, plunging into tall grass, my path hugging the fence. About midway between the sidewalk behind me and the alley ahead, I hit a seam in the fence where two panels are butted up against each other, but not joined. I look back towards the sidewalk. A few pedestrians cross to and fro, not looking in at me. In the alley there is no one. I attempt to lift a panel of the fence. It's heavy. Very heavy. I manage to budge it, but only a bit. It's going to be tough to move, but if I come back at night, I'll have dark on my side and can give it a lot more effort without being seen.

I take a photo with my phone and slip through to the alley. I look around at the other backs of buildings. The alley is half commercial and half residential. On the heritage home side, the row of townhouses on my right have covered parking. The small apartment building on the left has an entrance to an underground parking garage. Most of the windows have curtains drawn. No people are visible. The commercial buildings on the other side of the alley show fewer signs of life. Blinds shutter the small second floor windows that look down onto the heritage home's backyard. I will come back through the alley at night. No one will see me and no alarm will sound. My plan is set.

IT IS JUST after three a.m. My phone's vibration alarm woke me perfectly. The buzz on my nightstand was enough for me and only me. I trade my sweatpants for jeans and slip my phone in my pocket. The backpack has to stay behind; I can't afford baggage.

In the kitchen, I extract a butter knife from the cutlery drawer. I have no idea where Mariah keeps screwdrivers and other tools, which is probably on purpose, for reasons like this and who knows what other self-harm issues.

Slipping out the back door of Arbutus House is easy this time. There is no clumsy Rayanne to worry me and the confidence only experience can bring is on my side.

I wait until I'm down on Cornwall Avenue to call a cab. Buses don't run at this hour, but that's okay. After another refill from Mom, I now have over two hundred dollars in my account. I am armed with forty dollars in cash and if I spend more than half getting downtown, I can hit an ATM on the way back.

Staring down the dark orange-black road I flash back to my first escape, the moment when I ran from Mom, down to the highway in Surrey. I stared down a dark road that night too, willing transportation to rescue me before I got caught. Whatever Mom, Jane, or Dr. Werdiger might say, I am not addicted to this feeling. It's like I need to pee. This is not pleasant.

I finally see a yellow car coming down the road towards me. Only a few other cars have passed. I flag him down with excited waving and jumping. I don't care if he thinks I'm an idiot.

"Where to?" says the cab driver when I get into the back seat on the passenger side. I hope he isn't the chatty sort. I have no story prepared; only raw nerves pumping adrenaline through me, ramping me up for what I'm about to do.

"The corner of Barclay and Nicola, please. In the West End." I am jittery. I wonder if he can tell? Does he think I'm a junkie? Or a runaway? Technically, I am a runaway. Twice now.

The driver doesn't answer me. He simply shifts into Drive and pulls back out onto the road.

We drive in silence, which suits me fine. The slick dark road slides past us until we reach the bridge. The city glitters and vents steam across False Creek. The water's name is ironic; it reflects a fake version of a man-made world.

On the other side of the bridge, we turn left into the West End, and minutes later I am handing him a twenty-dollar bill. The charge is just over sixteen dollars, but I keep two dollars for change to be sure I can get home with the cash I have on hand.

I turn into the alley between Barclay and the retail-heavy street to the north. The heritage home is waiting for me, quietly fenced, shrouded in dark, but for the ambient light from the streetlights half a block away on either side.

I creep back to the small gap I started between the fence sections hours ago. In the dark, I am brave enough to heave with all my strength and move one of the panels inward. The gap is now large enough for me to squeeze through.

My butter knife comes out of my back pocket and I wedge it between the edge of the plywood and the windowsill on the side of the house. I pry and feel the knife start to bend. Damn it!

There is time. *Calm down*, I tell myself. I move on to one of the thick carpentry nails on the outside of the board. I work my knife under the head of the nail and pry and pry. It squeaks, but starts to move.

I move on to another nail. And another.

Now I can pry open the edge of the panel and wedge the handle of my knife between the board and the windowsill.

The ragged edges of the plywood scrape and cut my hands, but I pull. I alternate between prying with my knife handle and pulling with my bare hands.

The board gives way and pops off!

I do a quick scan of the alley and the yard around me. There is not a soul in sight. I put my foot on an old hydro meter on the side of the house. It's as solid as a rock. I climb up and in through the window, tearing several rips in my jeans on broken glass wedged into the bottom of the window sill.

I look down at my legs as my eyes adjust to the light. My jeans are ruined for anything except a rock concert. Blood seeps into the frayed white edges of the fresh tears in the fabric.

The cuts sting, but they don't look deep. I don't have time to assess for long. I need to be in and out. I have two stops to make. First, the fireplace to look for Akasha's letter.

I look around the room I'm in. It's a dining room, or was until the furniture was taken away and the fixtures gutted. Bits of trash are everywhere.

The next room is a kitchen, also gutted. Two giant gaps in the wall with ghostly stains around the edges hint at a fridge in the corner and stove between two cabinet panels.

So far, the house is unrecognizable as a home, let alone the century-old brothel from my dreams. As I pass through the entryway, something does seem familiar. A wood staircase heading to the second floor. Past that, I find what could have been a living room and a stripped-bare brick fireplace.

This could have been Calhoun's living room. Even if it was, the mantel where Akasha hid her letter has been completely torn away. Two weeks ago, two decades ago — it doesn't matter. If this *was* the right house, the letter is certainly gone.

I have a second stop to make. Akasha's old bedroom, if I can find it. I backtrack to the entryway and creep up the stairs as silently as I can. The upstairs level is small and dark. I move slowly, one step at a time.

I close my eyes and stand still. I picture the upstairs as it once was. I pause and breathe. Akasha's room was the first one on the left coming up from the kitchen stairs. That makes it the last one on the right now.

I open my eyes and feel along the wall. Dirt and leaves and random debris crunch lightly under my feet. I reach a dark opening and turn in passing through the doorway. Ambient light gives the room a faint yellow hue.

There is absolutely nothing but bits of trash in this

room. An old accordion-style closet door is partially open. I peek in the closet. A few piles of discarded plastic bags are clumped randomly.

I assess the room again. The rough shag carpet is filthy. I can see that even in the dark. The wallpaper is peeling everywhere and on the far wall it's peeled away enough to reveal layers underneath.

I peel back the top layer of stripes and find a plain, whitish layer underneath. There is a pattern behind that layer too, so I keep peeling. I reach the bottom layer and my lungs stop working, robbing me of my breath.

It could be a faint orange or pink; it's hard to tell. But the interlocking droplets dusted with gold are unmistakable.

I keep peeling until a huge section of the original wall-paper is visible. I take my knife and saw at the bottom of the bottom layer where it disappears under the crown molding running along the floor. I have to work hard with the blunt blade, but the old paper gives way and I lift it off the wall, peeling until a piece comes off in my hands. I slip it into my back pocket.

I take one last look around the room. I've been in the house long enough. It's time to go. I go down the back stairwell to the kitchen this time, back to the living room where the open window waits for me. I grab a piece of loose carpet and cover the jagged edges on the window sill. I hop down to the ground.

A flashlight flickers off in the alley. I wait a few beats

and then squeeze back through my opening in the construction fence. I leave the gap and walk back into the alley.

I round the corner and I'm face to face with a tall, beefy, middle-aged man in a uniform with a SECURITY patch sewn to his arm.

Chapter 26

*D*r. Werdiger has joined us in Jane's office. Mom is here as well, standing behind me.

"Young lady, the only reason we are sitting in my office and not talking to you through the bars of a jail cell is that I was able to convince the developer of that property that you are a mental health patient as well as a minor," says Jane.

"But I *am* a mental health patient *and* a minor," I say.

"You broke the law! This is not like running away or sneaking out to smoke. I got a call from the police in the middle of the night!" says Jane. I sense Mom's body tensing behind me.

"I thought it was just a rent-a-cop. And I didn't smoke. It was Rayanne," I say. I could add that the real reason we snuck out was to use my Ouija board more effectively, but I don't have to say the words out loud to know how much worse that would make things now.

"If that developer had wanted to press charges, you can be certain the police would have been their next call. Katelyn, you have a lot to learn about accountability and responsibility," says Jane.

Mom's continued silence is freaking me out, but I try to put her out of my mind. It's my counselor and psychiatrist I'm answering to at the moment.

"And Jane tells me your delusions regarding your past life and communicating with the dead are persisting, along with some kind of trance state which is occurring more frequently. Hearing voices, having recurring nightmares, and slipping into non-lucid states are serious symptoms. My recommendation is that we admit you back to BC Children's Hospital and begin a course of medication to complement your therapy. However, your mother does not wish us to medicate and instead is consenting to your release into her custody, provided that you remain in Vancouver for continued observation and treatment."

"Wait, I'm sorry to interrupt, but how am I going to stay in Vancouver if you're releasing me from Arbutus House? We can't afford to pay for a hotel for however long you think I still need treatment," I say with as much conviction as I can muster.

"You let me worry about what we can afford," says Mom coolly. "We're staying with Patty for a few weeks; longer, if needed."

"You will continue your treatment with me directly through regularly scheduled appointments until such time as I am ready to transfer you back to your psychiatrist in Nelson," says Dr. Werdiger. I look back at Mom. She remains silent with her arms crossed.

"Your job at Visions Vintage is over, as is your time at Arbutus House. After you leave this office, you will return to your bedroom, pack your things, and leave," says Jane.

Jane and Dr. Werdiger are both glaring at me. I feel like I've been sent to the principal's office, but no actual punishment is occurring. Although I've never been suspended, I wonder if this is what the experience is like: getting kicked out of somewhere you didn't want to be in the first place as extreme punishment for supposedly rotten behavior. I *was* wrong, though. I've never broken into anywhere in my life. I'll never do it again, but not because of this meeting. I already knew the difference between right and wrong. If they understood that Akasha was real and that she deserved justice — or closure at the very least — this would all look different to them.

"What were you thinking? Why were you there?" says Dr. Werdiger.

I turn around and look at Mom again. She nods, suggesting I should tell the truth. I consider the truth, briefly. Dr. Werdiger's frown changes my mind.

"It was a dare. A friend dared me to sneak in and stay for ten minutes. We were joking about the house being haunted and she dared me. That's all it was."

"Was one of the other girls in this house with you?" says Jane.

"No, it was a girl I met through Bryce. We had planned to meet downtown so she could watch me sneak into the house. She was behind me in the yard, waiting outside the construction fence. She must have seen me get caught and went the other way."

"What was the other girl's name?" says Jane.

"I'm not giving you her name. It's not fair to get her in trouble when she didn't really do anything anyway."

"Okay, I don't think there's much value in hashing this out any further today," says Mom as she steps forward.

"Please call my office at your earliest convenience to schedule an appointment for Katelyn," says Dr. Werdiger. He passes a business card to Mom, who forces a smile and tucks it into her wallet.

"Katelyn, go pack your things," says Mom.

In my bedroom I am alone for the first time since the Barclay house. I carefully extract the wallpaper from my back pocket. I pluck my diary from its hiding spot and open it to the front page. I place the wallpaper piece inside and close the book again before wedging it into the front section of my backpack.

It takes me less than ten minutes to scour my bedroom and stuff every one of my personal possessions into my bag. I acquired a few outfits from Visions, but not much more. My bag is practically bursting at the seams, but I manage to get the zipper closed.

I say quick goodbyes to Mariah and Melody, both of whom seem disinterested. Therese and Yolanda are at the community center. Mariah promises to say goodbye for me. Bonds formed in situations like Arbutus House should be strong, reinforced by common ground. That's not how I feel walking out the door. I will never see these girls again. I won't try to contact them and they won't try to find me, online or off.

I get into Mom's car with an uneasy sense that I've forgotten something, but the feeling fades. I look back as we drive away. The yard is empty. What did I expect? They'd change their tune and be standing outside, smiling and waving?

"So why did you really break into that house? I looked up the address and took a drive past it. Patty told me she took you for a walk in the West End. What were you looking for?" asks Mom.

"I was looking for some small scrap of evidence that Akasha was real."

"And what did you find?"

I remember my piece of wallpaper. I want to show it to Mom, but that precious piece of paper is for my eyes only. It's not proof of anything other than that the house is over a hundred years old.

"Katelyn?"

"Nothing. I didn't find anything. The place had been renovated over and over and stripped bare long before I got there. It was a stupid idea. I had another dream about Akasha and I was desperate." If I explain my ability to channel Akasha in my diary has grown by leaps and bounds, Mom will be furious. I'm going to stick with the term *dream* from now on.

"Next time you have a dream about Akasha or find her writing in your diary, just tell me. Talk to me about it."

"I will. I've already said the break-in was stupid. It's over and done. I won't do it again."

"Okay, I believe you. How about we grab a couple of burgers? Sound good?"

"That sounds perfect."

After a trip through the drive-thru of the nearest burger joint, we park in front of Patty's small, rectangular home. Mom calls it a "Vancouver Special" although it doesn't seem like much of a gem to me. Just plain and overpriced.

Inside, Patty has already re-made her couch into a bed with fresh sheets and pillows. Mom had been sleeping on the couch, but tonight, Patty wants the couch so she can give Mom and me her bed. Patty insists, but this does not make Mom happy.

"Tomorrow I'm going to finally sort out the clutter in my spare room. It's full of boxes and useless junk. I'm embarrassed I hadn't gotten around to it when Becky first got here," says Patty.

"Thank you again, Patty, I can't tell you enough how grateful we are," says Mom as she shoots me a back-me-up-kid glare.

"Yes, thank you, Patty."

"We won't be here very long. I want Katelyn to get the best care possible, but I'm starting to lose patience with the counselor and the doctor involved. We've got an appointment with Dr. Werdiger tomorrow. If he doesn't come up with something useful, I'm taking Katelyn back home. I don't care if he disagrees," says Mom.

"Don't get mad, Mom, it's not their fault. It's nobody's fault. I'm too weird to fix."

"Katelyn, you don't need to be fixed. And you are both welcome to stay here as long as you like. Everything will sort itself out. You'll see." Patty's confidence shines in stark contrast to Mom's irritation. I hope something good happens at the hospital tomorrow.

Chapter 27

Patty has hauled half her spare room into the back hallway by the time Mom and I are finishing our breakfast cereal.

"We're heading off to Children's Hospital now, Patty," Mom calls back into the dense tunnel of cardboard boxes.

Patty's head pops into the opening she left to get back to the rest of the house.

"I'd say have fun, but that's probably not the right thing. How about, good luck?"

"I'm going to drop Katelyn off at that art class afterwards and putter around Main Street while she's there. We'll be home for dinner."

"Thanks again for the classes, Patty," I add. I thanked Patty before, but Mom hadn't heard me. I need every extra brownie point I can get right now.

BC Children's Hospital is quiet this afternoon. Since I don't have a room for Dr. Werdiger to visit me in, I'm in a waiting room sitting under large letters that spell *Pediatric Psychiatry*.

"Katelyn Medena, the doctor is ready to see you now," says a slim, short girl who doesn't look much older than me.

"Hello, Katelyn!" says Dr. Werdiger brightly as we enter the consultation room.

"Uh, hi," I say awkwardly. His happiness confuses me. Mom stays silent.

"I have some great news. I've been able to get Katelyn in for a CT scan. It took some doing, but I think we may get some information we can finally act on."

"What's a CT scan?" I ask. I have a feeling I'm not going to like his answer.

"It's nothing to be afraid of. Think of a lot of very accurate x-rays being compiled by a computer with state-of-the-art precision."

"Why do you want to scan my daughter's head? What are you looking for?"

"Mom, isn't this what you wanted from the beginning?"

"Katelyn!" Mom looks at me with a mixture of hurt and worry in her mossy eyes.

"At this point, I'm ready to rule out mental health issues, a bit of bad behavior aside. I've reviewed Jane's notes and I've met with Katelyn myself. Becky, I think you might have been right all along in suspecting a physical issue here."

Mom and I are both looking at Dr. Werdiger with amazement. He's speaking as though my brain holds a passing curiosity for him.

"What physical issues are you going to find with a scan?" I can see the anxiety building behind Mom's wide eyes.

"I won't speculate needlessly. As I said, there's no reason to be afraid. This is just one last point on a check-list so we can all know we've been thorough." Dr. Werdiger has gone into damage control mode, pushing down an invisible barrier to calm Mom.

"How long do we have to wait? I'm hoping to take Katelyn home to Nelson as soon as possible," says Mom. She is using her breath to calm herself, I can see it.

"Wednesday. The day after tomorrow. Normally the wait could be a few weeks to a few months depending on other health variables. But I pushed the urgency, knowing how long you've already been away from home."

"Thank you, we appreciate that. I think another couple of days will be fine."

"Katelyn, do you have any objections?" says Dr. Werdiger.

"Nope. Scan me. Poke me. Prod me. I'm good, as long as I get to go home afterwards." I look at Mom and smile to show her I'm not afraid. She smiles back and puts her arm around me. I think she's supporting herself more than me. I don't blame her, though.

MOM TAKES ME to art class as promised. Today's session is an assignment on positive and negative space. Mr. Macpherson (aka Reese) has dimmed the lights. On the table, he's placed a plastic ball with holes all over it under a spotlight lamp. We are supposed to represent the light areas with charcoal, leaving the dark shadows

blank on the page. We will end up with abstract drawings that don't look like anything, but I don't mind. The
scene at the center of the room isn't interesting enough
to inspire a project I'd want to keep.

I draw the light shapes over and over and over. I am
bored after the third attempt, so under the cover of dark,
I try something for myself. I close my eyes and picture the
locket I saw when hypnotically visualizing my treasure.

I look at the locket in my mind, assessing the edges,
the pattern etched onto the cover. I open my eyes and
recreate the shape on my page. I try to add details, but
the charcoal is too messy. I draw the shape again. I draw
it once more with the middle piece open. I draw until I
have half a dozen egg-shaped lockets on my page. I still
can't capture enough detail.

I tear the page away and pull my number two pencil
from my case. I start another version of the locket. This
time I add detail. Even in the dimmed light, I add details
I feel I know like the back of my hand. The more I draw
the pendant, the more I feel like I've run my fingers over
its subtle shape and felt the texture of each carved mark.
Suddenly the overhead light comes on.

"That's all the time we have today. I hope everyone
found the project very 'illuminating' in terms of how we
see light and shadow," says Reese.

"Ha ha. I see what you did there," says the round
grandmother I've sat next to twice now.

"My son tells me he loves my 'dad jokes,' so I thought

I'd share one with you," says Reese. "Now, everyone, please turn in your best work from this afternoon's session. And I'll see you again after the weekend."

I leave my classmate shaking her head and I tear away a corner square of my top sketch sheet. I gently slip the pencil drawing of Akasha's locket into my pencil case. I select a charcoal sketch and hand it in. Mom is waiting for me outside; I run to her car like the end of a normal school day and I feel a small sliver of normality return.

PATTY ORDERED PIZZA for us shortly after we got back. I wish we were all enjoying a vacation and not some distorted visit brought about by my fascination with a suspected past life. It might not be "suspected" in my own mind — I know what I know — but it's obvious that what I know doesn't mean anything outside my own head.

After a few slices, I excuse myself for a bath. I was never allowed to have one at Arbutus House. They had a somewhat morbid "No Baths" policy that also banned shaving and sharp objects. Patty's bathroom is just a normal one, so I can bring my diary along and try to write. I'd like to add something normal to the mess of the last few months. Especially if I'm going to be commenting on a head scan soon.

Once I'm lying back in the tub, I'm just not interested in writing. It's hard to pass on the chance for guaranteed privacy, so I pick up my diary anyway. And before I know it, the involuntary swoops of my ballpoint pen have started again.

Earlier today, Mr. Calhoun took me back to the shop where Sanjay works. He could have told me and I would have believed him, but instead he chose to show me. At first, I thought we were going on another of our outings. Mr. Calhoun has taken to bringing me for walks and small errands. I expect he believes he is endearing himself to me.

We returned to Sanjay's place of work for a special reason. Mr. Hasan was not there. Whether he simply no longer works there or has returned to India, I could not say. For a few short minutes, I thought Mr. Calhoun was relenting in his insistence that I sell my body in his house. I thought there was a chance he had brought me to Sanjay to reunite us. I tried to step off the sidewalk to cross the street and Mr. Calhoun grabbed my arm. And then I saw that Sanjay had a different co-worker. She could be called pretty, if not a bit plain. She was about my age. She wore a light blue sari and had a braid longer than mine. I could hear the tinkle of the gold bells on her scarf. Had it been a wedding present? Probably.

I knew this woman was Sanjay's bride from the way they looked at each other. He looked at her the way he used to look at me. How it was possible, I can't say. I will never look at another man the way I looked at Sanjay. Yet, there he stood, admiring the other girl as though I had never existed. And to him, I have been dead for months. He believes me to be at the bottom of Vancouver Harbor.

While I watched, they worked moving boxes and packets around the shop, looking up to smile at each other intermittently. Sanjay walked past her, pausing to take her hand and kiss her lightly on the lips. There could be no question. The match he came to Canada for had certainly taken place. I could reveal myself and it would make no difference. Sanjay was far too honorable to abandon a woman he had married. I would only bring him more sadness and regret.

My grief today knows no bounds. Nothing can happen to me now to make me more miserable than I am at this moment. I have lost my love. I can only now wonder what horrible deed of a past life I am now atoning for in this one.

Chapter 28

I finally feel the lazy days of summer vacation now that I'm at Patty's house. I can get up when I want to. I don't have a schedule or rigid rules to follow. If it weren't for Akasha's sad news about Sanjay's marriage, I would be in great spirits this morning.

In Patty's spare room, I have some privacy, so I decide to write to Akasha. If Jane suggested it, maybe writing to her really is good for me, although I'm sure an ongoing conversation isn't what Jane had in mind.

Akasha,

To say that this has been a strange summer is a wild understatement. I have never been more on edge or more determined. I think this adventure has brought out good qualities in me. That's bizarre, isn't it? Which is saying something, coming from me.

I'm supposed to be finding closure for you, but I haven't been as successful as I'd hoped. I've done everything I can, but I have to move on. It's time for me to go home and that might mean I can't uncover more about what happened to you. I'm so sorry. I know you reached out to me to get some kind of justice and I failed you.

I wish your life had been happier. I wish you'd gotten the life you deserved. I know this will be too little, too late, but if it brings you any comfort, know that I'm never going to stop believing and I'll never stop trying to prove you were real or that you were murdered. There may not be consequences left for Mr. Calhoun in this life, but I hope wherever you are, you're with Sanjay. If it works like that. Or are you trapped in my head with me? I guess I may never understand how this works.

Goodbye, for now.

While Patty is at work, Mom and I spend the day watching TV and meandering around the neighborhood. There is a corner grocery and a small playground nearby. I feel like I'm getting too old for playgrounds, but until the term "teen" is in my official age, I feel like I can get away with a bag of gummy bears and a leisurely swing session.

Mom lies back on the grass and watches the few fluffy clouds in the sky. She seems to have relaxed, almost as though she's been on vacation.

We're back in the house watching yet another movie when Patty gets home from work. I stay lazy on the couch while Mom and Patty spend over an hour covering the tiny table in homemade Mexican food. We're having tacos and enchiladas alongside generous portions of guacamole, bean dip, fresh salsa, and warm tortilla chips. Normally, Mom would insist I help, on principle alone, but Patty's small kitchen makes this principle hard to enforce.

I watch the small table fill quickly and it occurs to me this is a table for one, occasionally two people. I wonder, would Patty have been happier with a family of her own? Even Mom and I have each other.

"I think we're going to have to eat in the living room tonight. We made too much food!" says Mom.

"It's just this table. I've toyed around with getting something bigger, but it's a small house and an even smaller kitchen," says Patty.

"I think it's great. And the food looks great too," I say with genuine energy.

"Well then, dig in, ladies!" says Patty.

Mom and I are both making plates, but Patty hangs back.

"Before we get too full to think, I have something I need to tell you both," says Patty. Tingles run from my tailbone to the back of my neck. Instinct tells me this is bad news.

"Patty, I hear sheepishness in your voice," says Mom.

"There's a reason for that. I don't want you to get angry, but I took a liberty I think is best for everyone," says Patty.

"God, Patty, what have you done?" says Mom.

I am no longer dishing food on my plate. Steam passes

up from it through my peripheral vision. I won't take my eyes off Patty.

"I called the Manns yesterday while you were at the hospital."

"What would possess you to do that?" Mom is both angry and shocked. I'm curious.

"When you told me what Professor Mann said to Katelyn, I couldn't get over it. Who speaks to a child that way? And with so little provocation! I thought everyone involved deserved a little closure before you go back to the Kootenays."

"So, what exactly is happening?" I chime in.

"The Manns are coming over tomorrow afternoon to clear the air. Bryce's mother agrees with me that the kids should have a chance to stay friends, regardless of what his father is so worked up over." Patty's confidence is less than convincing. Mom's glare isn't helping.

"Is Professor Mann coming with them?" I ask quickly.

"I really don't think this is going to help anyone," says Mom.

"But will Katelyn be any worse off? There's no chance she'll be alone with that man. If anything, she'll get the apology she richly deserves. Bryce's mother was mortified at the whole thing. She didn't really know the extent of what happened until I told her. What kind of communication that marriage has, I can only imagine," says Patty.

"It's none of our business!" says Mom, loudly.

"I never want to see Professor Mann again for the rest of my life. He scared the hell out me." I pause, choosing my words. "But I really miss Bryce. He's still my best friend. We didn't do anything wrong anyway. I didn't deserve to get told off, or to have my friend taken away. Maybe I should take my chances with an angry father rather than lose my friend forever."

"It's your call, sweetie. We can cancel whatever arrangements Patty made and nobody will think less of you."

"Thanks, Mom, but I want to give it a try. And thanks, Patty. I know you're doing this because you care." I take a decisive bite of my enchilada and give them both a goofy full-mouth smile. Mom shakes her head and gives one last hard look to Patty, but we're all finally eating in peace.

I'm tired after dinner, so I excuse myself and go to bed early. My second night on this cot is not proving more enjoyable than the first. No wonder Mom didn't want the spare room. Privacy is less valuable when you're uncomfortable. Still, I feel sleep creeping up like a thick fog.

I AWAKE IN a strange room with a towering ceiling and a light murmur of voices around me. My chest is heavy and tight. I try to lift my head to look around, but I am too weak. I catch sight of Mr. Calhoun speaking with a woman in a white dress with a white cap. I must be in a hospital. Have I been beaten? I lift my hand to my face and touch gingerly. Nothing is tender.

"Her treatment and progress are of no interest to me. She is not in my care, nor is she any relation or concern of mine. She was a guest in my home and at the first sign of consumption, I brought her here," says Mr. Calhoun. He is not attempting to lower his voice for my benefit.

"Sir, please, if she has no relations nearby, that is reason to continue your interest in her care," says the nurse. She is speaking quietly, but I can just make out her words.

"Be clear on this; if you require funds to treat her, you will not receive a penny from me. Throw her back on the street. That's where I found her and likely where she belongs. I'll not have her spreading this sickness in my house."

"I can see the girl is awake. If you'd like to say good bye, now might be the time." The nurse is looking at Mr. Calhoun with pleading eyes. He looks at me with disgust, and then back at the nurse with the same expression. He turns and leaves without another word. The nurse approaches me.

"Hello, dear, how are you feeling?"

"I feel like a load of bricks fell on my chest. What happened to —" a fit of coughing suddenly hits me and the nurse passes me a cotton handkerchief. I take my hand away to receive the cloth. My palm is covered in blood.

"You have tuberculosis. It is a condition of the lungs. You'll need to rest if you're to make a recovery."

"What —" I stop again, feeling the urge to cough. I cover my mouth with the stained cloth.

"Rest now, dear."

I lie back on the bed and close my eyes. A few moments pass and I hear the nurse's hushed voice again.

"Yes, doctor?" His first response is inaudible, but then he adds, "No, her case is quite advanced. She may have contracted the disease before leaving India. Or on the steamship you mentioned." The nurse mutters something about "time" and the doctor speaks again. "Two weeks, maybe three."

I'm horrified. This doctor is talking about how much time I have left to live.

Chapter 29

*M*y alarm clock tells me it is nine-fifteen in the morning. My windowless room is lit only by ambient daylight from the hallway. The house is quiet. I know Patty will have left over an hour ago, so the clatter and clink sounds in the distance must be Mom.

I retrieve my hair elastic from my end table nightstand and tie back my messy hair. I want to stay in my room to decompress, but I need the bathroom. And I'm hungry. It will be hard not to tell Mom about last night's dream, but I'll have to try.

Akasha died of natural causes — more specifically, a disease. So what am I doing chasing some kind of justice or closure for her? What could Akasha possibly want from me? A locket? My former self must have been a sentimental drama queen to go to so much trouble over recovering a piece of jewelry. It has to be something else. But what?

"Katelyn, it's time to get ready. We need to be back at the hospital by ten-fifteen. They need to prep you for the ten-thirty scan," says Mom, calling down the hall from the kitchen.

I'm dressed with my hair in a loose ponytail moments later. Mom shoves a dry bowl of cereal at me and points out a milk carton on the counter. We're in the car before nine-thirty.

Re-entering the BC Children's Hospital feels routine today. We know where we're going; Mom scouted out the Department of Radiology before.

We check in and I'm ushered to an examination room where I change into a white gown covered in pink teddy bears. I really am in a children's hospital. I sneak a quick glance in the mirror while I retie my ponytail. My baby blue eyes look darker for a moment. I blink and my irises are normal again.

Dr. Werdiger is nowhere in sight, but a nurse is waiting to take me to a dark room with a long shell-like bed with a huge white ring behind it. A small cupped pillow marks where I'll rest my head. She asks me to lie down and helps me into the right position. Now I'm scared.

"Try not to move while we're doing the scan. Lie as still as you can. Don't worry about the odd finger twitch or your breathing, but if you shift or move your body, the head will move as well and we won't get a clear picture," says the nurse.

"Don't worry. I'm scared stiff. There's no danger of me moving."

"It'll be over before you know it." The nurse touches my arm and smiles before retreating to a desk in the corner.

I hear a long beep. And then nothing. Then the bed lifts a few inches and slides backward, inserting me into the white ring. I open my eyes for a moment and it feels like I'm inside a huge donut. The bed moves again gently and I try not to flinch, snapping my eyes shut instead. I am moved back again, forward again, and then the lights come on.

"We're all done. You can chat with your doctor to get the results," says the nurse.

She leads me back to the examination room and tells me to dress. As soon as I'm back in my T-shirt and jeans, a knock on the door startles me. The nurse comes in before I can answer.

"Dr. Werdiger would like you to wait here for the results."

"What about my mom? Where is she?"

"I'll send her in." The nurse is gone as quickly as she barged in.

Mom replaces her a few minutes later.

"I thought we weren't going to get these results until we got home to Nelson," says Mom.

"I guess he's got time for us today," I say, just as confused.

As we wait in silence, thoughts start to bubble up through my brain. Maybe Dr. Werdiger wants to talk to us right away because something bad came up on the scan. Something bad and urgent. What could be so important he can't wait to talk to us?

"Mom, do you think we'd get in trouble if we just left anyway?"

"I don't think we'd get in trouble, but we'd probably have to come back. Doctors don't usually give test results over the phone."

"Maybe he got sidetracked somewhere," she adds. I can see she's getting nervous too. We scroll away on our phones for a while. I close the blog I was reading and check the time. It's past noon. We've been waiting for almost an hour.

A knock at the door finally comes.

"Sorry for the wait, ladies. Okay, I've got good news and bad news," Dr. Werdiger says casually as he steps into our fear-filled closet of an exam room.

"What?" Mom clamps her hand over her mouth. I can see from Dr. Werdiger's demeanor that it's not that grim, but "bad news" is all Mom heard him say.

"Sorry, Mrs. Medena, I shouldn't have put it like that. What I meant to say is that Katelyn's scan is normal. The bad news is that we don't have fresh insight as to what might be troubling her. I'm going to recommend continued appointments with your original psychiatrist in Nelson. And if you see any other indications of fugue states or otherwise not lucid waking incidents, please contact a medical professional immediately."

"But she's okay?"

"He just said that, Mom." She shoots me a glare but there's more relief in her eyes than anger.

"Yes, she's fine."

Mom hugs me.

"All right. Let's get home and pack," says Mom.

I think briefly of our narrow old house back in Nelson.

And then I remember our date with the Mann family.

Chapter 30

*P*atty's house is immaculate when Mom and I walk through the door. A spread of fruit, cheese, crackers, vegetables, and several pitchers of juice has been arranged thoughtfully on her tiny table and kitchen counter. Her nicest glass tumblers and stacks of napkins and small white plates are waiting for us as well. A few padded folding chairs have been added to the living room. I recognize them from Patty's back hall as having been stashed in her spare room.

The scene warms my heart and makes me angry at the same time. Patty has tried her best to be hospitable and I can perfectly picture the sneer on Professor Mann's face when he walks in. I won't say a word to Patty, though.

"Patty, you've been busy!" says Mom. She smiles broadly while combing her hands through her auburn curls. She doesn't know Professor Mann very well, either.

"Best foot forward, right? I know our family meeting is going to go well, but it doesn't hurt to set the stage," says Patty.

I smile as enthusiastically as I can, but no words of false hope come to mind. A rapping on the glass panel of Patty's screen door halts my train of thought.

Behind Mom and me stands the entire Mann family: the Professor and Radhika with Bryce and Mitchell behind them. I hadn't noticed that Mitchell is nearly as tall as his father. I must have overestimated Professor Mann's height. Radhika's ironed hair and perfectly drawn maroon lips complement her silky cream blouse. Professor Mann is wearing a crisp pale blue collared shirt and dark denim — very informal for him.

"Good afternoon! Welcome! Please come in," says Patty as she steps around Mom and opens her outer door.

"Hello. Thank you so much for having us," says Radhika. Professor Mann remains silent.

"Hey," says Bryce to me. He smiles and it's like a rush of cool water relieving a sunburn. Maybe the worst is over and everything is all right.

"Radhika, it's so lovely to see you. And you too, Bryce." Mom extends her smile to Professor Mann and Mitchell as well.

"Ladies, I'm going to excuse myself," says Professor Mann, addressing Mom and Patty, getting blank stares in return. "But not before I apologize to Katelyn." I am struck dumb by the idea.

"My tone and conduct last week were not appropriate. I've since discussed this matter with my wife and son. I see no reason why the children can't maintain their friendship through emails or other correspondence. But I can't condone what my wife is about to disclose.

I want no part of it. I'll wait in the car."

"I'm coming with you, Dad," says Mitchell. This is just as well as far as I'm concerned, although now the clock is ticking on our visit. Professor Mann won't want to wait very long.

"Oh, uh, sure. That's ..." Patty is still processing, looking at her lovely snack arrangement.

"Let's have a seat," says Mom, gesturing towards Patty's sofa. Radhika and Bryce sit down. Mom and I sit in the folding chairs facing them on the other side of the coffee table.

"Where to start?" says Radhika. She opens her clutch and scoops her hand inside. My heart lurches. A gold oval locket! The metal has a pattern etched on the front. It could be Akasha's!

"Bryce confided in me about some of what Katelyn's been going through the last few months. I wasn't entirely surprised; I hope you won't take that the wrong way. My dear, you have always been a sensitive little soul." Radhika smiles warmly at me, and then looks to my mom.

"I thought I was assisting Katelyn with a summer school project, helping her do some research on the *Komagata Maru*. Because my great-grandfather was on that boat, I turned up what I could find to help her out."

As Radhika speaks, my heart is pounding in my ears. I look at Bryce. He's blushing, but not from looking at me. He looks embarrassed by what his mother is saying.

"I got interested again myself, so I continued looking

through everything my mother saved from her father's journey to Canada. Among my family photos and letters, I found this locket. Bryce told me Katelyn had been looking for a locket because she believes another girl's spirit is looking for it. I can't say what this means, but I've always wondered why my grandfather kept a locket with his photo … and a girl who isn't my grandmother." Radhika opens the locket and passes it to Mom.

"I don't know what to say." Mom examines the photos in the locket. My chest is so tight I can barely breathe as she passes it to me.

"It's them!" I blurt, before clamping my hand over my mouth. I look around the room at every face staring at me. I look back at the locket. I haven't seen Akasha or Sanjay's faces anywhere but my dreams.

A closer look at Sanjay sends a flash of pins and needles through my limbs. The wheels in my head all lock into place at that moment. Akasha doesn't want justice or her locket. She wants Bryce. She wants Sanjay back!

"Can I see that?" Patty reaches towards the locket and instinctively I pass it to her.

"Careful though, it's a family heirloom," says Radhika. Bryce is looking even more humiliated. Patty examines the open locket, but quickly returns it to Radhika, who closes it and pops it back in her clutch.

"Sorry, I know this is weird," I say to Bryce. "Wait, there's something else!" I run to my makeshift bedroom and fish my drawings out of my backpack.

"They're not great, but they're as close as I could get without having her model for me." I pass the drawings to Radhika, who examines them with interest. "Here's the locket too." I pass the last sketch over.

"Can this possibly get more bizarre?" says Bryce. He scratches his carefully gelled messy bangs.

"Have some fruit, hon. There's juice too," says Patty. She rises to start a plate for him, still a caregiver at heart.

"Are you able to scan these for me? Or make some photocopies? Bryce can give you our mailing address," says Radhika.

"I'd love to do that. This is weird. I spent half the summer shut in a group home just for talking about this. Now it's … real," I say, unable to conceal my disbelief. I know this turn will bother Mom.

"Sweetie, that's not why we had you there," says Mom. I wonder who the "we" is in her mind. She shoves her hand back into her curls and leaves it there for a moment while she thinks.

"You thought there was something wrong. I know that. It's okay," I say flatly.

"As much as I'd like to explore this strange connection a little more, we do need to get going." Radhika rises and Bryce sets his plate of fruit on the counter.

"We'll keep in touch. I promise. Dad's not going to freak out again, and if he does, Mom's got my back," says Bryce.

Radhika opens the front door with her smooth, graceful

arm. Bryce is following her, but pauses to look at me. I take a chance and grab him for a hug. I have to reach up now that he's nearly a foot taller than me. And it's goofy having our mothers watching us, but I won't see him for who knows how long. Professor Mann certainly won't be bringing him back to the Kootenays for visits.

"I miss you already. But I'm glad we're going to stay friends," I say, still hanging on. Bryce is hugging back, which I know is awkward for him.

"Don't worry. It's all good," says Bryce. A hint of a crack in his voice tugs at my heart. He pulls away and I let go.

"Thank you again for having us," says Radhika. She smiles and starts off down Patty's front steps.

Bryce follows, but when he reaches the sidewalk, he turns back to wave. He grins and his brown eyes light up. I wave back and I watch as the Manns' black suv pulls away from the curb and speeds off down the street.

Chapter 31

*T*he air smells like burnt leaves for the first time this fall as I walk home from school. Wind pulls at a few loose strands at the top of my braid; I've started wearing my hair just like Akasha did. My denim jacket is not quite warm enough today. The weather has turned for the year.

I round the corner on to my street thinking about how satisfying it feels to step on a perfectly crisp dry leaf and watch it crumble to pieces under my foot. It's almost as good as popping bubble wrap.

I turn up the concrete path to my front stairs and see a small manila parcel on the welcome mat at the center of our veranda. I smile knowing that in Nelson, even a downtown adjacent street like mine is safe enough to leave a parcel on the step — unlike my summer accommodation in Vancouver.

The parcel has writing in black felt marker. As soon as I see my name, I recognize Bryce's handwriting. I sit down on the porch swing and work my fingernail into the corner of the parcel, prying up the seal. The fact that Bryce has remembered my birthday is reason enough to celebrate. Whatever he's put in this parcel is incidental.

Inside layers of tissue paper are taped frustratingly tight. I tear and tear shredding the tissue until I get to the lump at the heart of the package. There is a piece of paper taped around the outside of the small cardboard box. A letter, no doubt.

I carefully peel up one corner of the tape to free the piece of paper. It's an envelope. I've always been the kind of kid to open the present before the card — unless Mom is standing over my shoulder to make me follow etiquette. Today I'm alone, so the box comes first, no contest. I work the cardboard lid up off the bottom of the box and reveal a brassy-gold egg-shaped pendant on a patina-stained chain. Is this what I think it is?

I pick up the pendant and, sure enough, there is a small, flat disk in the middle that I can push out on a hinge to reveal two photos. Akasha and Sanjay, right where I left them in Vancouver. I may never get further proof that Akasha is part of my cosmic past, but I know it in my heart and that's what matters to me.

Now I need to read the letter. If he's giving me Akasha's locket, Radhika consented. This letter better tell me why.

Vancouver, October 22nd

Hey Katelyn,
I wanted this to be a surprise. I hope you're reading this
with a smile on your face. Mom sat on the fence for a

while before I finally convinced her that this locket is really yours. She believed me, but she just didn't want to part with it. She's all gushy talking about us being destined to meet and ... well, she's a romantic at heart.

Anyway, I promised her you'll take care of it. Wear it if you want to, but I hope you'll think of me whenever you look at it. Mom says I look just like my great-great-grandfather. It's hard to say for sure with an old photo and such an old-fashioned look.

I'm still hoping to come back to Nelson with Mom in the spring. I know it's a long time. I guess we're lucky we've got email and Skype. Text me when you get this so we can do a call.

Love,

Bryce

I don't waste a moment before fastening the clasp at the back of my neck. The tiny click feels like that triumphant moment when you fit in the last piece in a very large and complicated puzzle.

Historical Background

The story of Katelyn Medena and her connection to a girl named Akasha from early twentieth-century India is completely fictional. The context of the story, however, has roots in actual historical events.

On May 23, 1914, the steamship SS *Komagata Maru* arrived in Vancouver and attempted to dock in Coal Harbour. Of the 376 passengers seeking entry into Canada, only twenty-four were admitted. The 352 weary passengers forced to return to India faced military action from the British when they arrived in Kolkata, then Calcutta. In the chaos and violence that followed, nineteen people were killed, while most of the rest were arrested and faced years of imprisonment.

There are a few key points in *Secrets from Myself* that are worth noting with reference to the historical *Komagata Maru* incident.

Katelyn has very little information when she begins her research into Akasha's life and times. Through a diary entry from Akasha, Katelyn's first piece of "evidence" is that the girl's point of origin was the Indian province of Punjab. Katelyn later learns that the ship Akasha came to Canada on was called the *Komagata Maru*, a name many readers might recognize as Japanese. The official point of departure for the ship's 1914 trip to Vancouver was Hong Kong.

The discrepancy between the potential immigrants' citizenship and their point of departure for Canada was the grounds used for barring their entry. The law, known as the continuous journey regulation, was enacted in 1908. While conducting historical research at Vancouver's Central Library, Katelyn also learns that while most passengers on the Komagata Maru were from the Sikh faith, there were also Hindu and Muslim people on board. At the time, Canada was more welcoming to Christian Europeans, hence the exclusionary and unjust continuous journey regulation.

Katelyn's geographic search for Akasha in Vancouver initially takes her to Crab Park, east of Gastown. As mentioned above, the *Komagata Maru* was held in Coal Harbour, which was and is located to the west of Crab Park, separated by iconic Canada Place. Because Katelyn has so little information, she simply gravitates towards the bright orange cranes operating at today's Port of Vancouver.

On May 23, 2008, the BC Legislative Assembly unanimously passed a resolution apologizing for the *Komagata Maru* incident.

On August 3, 2008, Prime Minister Stephen Harper apologized for the *Komagata Maru* incident at the thirteenth annual Ghadri Babiyan Da Mela festival in Surrey, BC.

On May 18, 2016, Prime Minister Justin Trudeau formally apologized in the House of Commons for the injustice and suffering resulting from Canadian laws and officials' actions during the *Komagata Maru* incident.

Acknowledgements

Thanks to my mom for being my first and most trusted beta reader. And thanks to my sister Sarah for letting me quiz her on plot ideas while she's wearing her teacher's hat.

Many of the historical references would not have been possible without the detailed records on the Simon Fraser University Library's website, *Komagata Maru: Continuing the Journey*, which can be found at komagatamaru journey.ca.

Last, but not least, extra special thanks to my friend Nivrita for helping me include a bit of Hindi text in the story.

About the Author

Christine Hart has an undergraduate degree in writing in literature, and has worked in corporate communications and design. She has written many books for middle grade, young adult, and new adult audiences, including *Watching July* (a Moonbeam Awards Gold Medal recipient and a Westchester Fiction Awards winner); *Best Laid Plans*; *Stalked*; and the Variant Conspiracy series.